Bool
Fine

CROSS OF IRON

Reverend Matthew Devlin is busy writing the moment six desperadoes burst through the church doors, attacking both him and his wife Sarah. When Matt regains consciousness, he's been trussed to his own cross, and Sarah has been viciously murdered. And so Matt, an ex-bounty hunter, must once again take the path of violence to exact retribution for those who have sinned against man and his Maker. With an old rival also on the trail of the gang, a confrontation between good and evil is inevitable. But who will emerge the victor?

ETHAN FLAGG

CROSS OF IRON

Complete and Unabridged

LINFORD
Leicester

First published in Great Britain in 2017 by
Robert Hale
an imprint of The Crowood Press
Wiltshire

First Linford Edition
published 2020
by arrangement with
The Crowood Press
Wiltshire

A catalogue record for this book is available
from the British Library.

ISBN 978–1–4448–4472–6

Published by
Ulverscroft Limited
Anstey, Leicestershire

Set by Words & Graphics Ltd.
Anstey, Leicestershire
Printed and bound in Great Britain by
T. J. International Ltd., Padstow, Cornwall

This book is printed on acid-free paper

Breakthrough

Jack Patch, along with five of his men, were camped in a secluded draw two miles west of Willcox, Arizona. It was late on a Friday afternoon on the last day of July. All of them except the gang leader were splayed out around the fire, drinking coffee and smoking roll-ups. The youngest member of the gang, Klute, was avidly devouring a lurid and well-thumbed dime novel.

Only Patch was on his feet. Striding up and down, his singular gaze kept drifting towards the narrow entrance to the draw. He was not the most patient of men. Hanging around like this did not sit well with one-eyed Jack. 'What's keeping that guy?' he asked for the umpteenth time.

1

'Give him a chance, boss,' a lean-limbed jasper called Greylag answered, laying a month-old newssheet aside. 'He's only been gone a couple of hours. And we want the survey done properly, don't we?'

'If'n there's one guy can get in there and find the safest way to lift that strong box, it's Gentleman Jim Smollett,' remarked Blackie Hayes. The heavy set rough neck then added a further outlook to the blunt conversation. 'He might be a touch on the snooty side, but ain't the guy always done the business since you took him on?'

Patch relaxed. 'Guess you're right, boys. I just hate this waiting around. It sets my nerves on edge.'

The man in question was at that very moment on his way back from Willcox. Clad in his regulation black suit and necktie, Jim Smollett was well satisfied that his recce of the Wells Fargo Express Office had been so highly profitable. Not only was the place closed all weekend, but the premises immediately adjacent were empty.

Gentleman Jim had been forced on to the owl-hooter trail after being caught with his fingers in the till while employed as a cashier at the New Mexico branch of the First National Bank in Farmington. He had escaped a hefty jail term by skipping bail and the territory days before his trial.

Jim's knowledge of the banking profession had come to the attention of Jack Patch when the two unlikely associates met by chance in Flagstaff.

Some rowdy cowpokes were hassling the stylish dude at the bar of the Eagle's Nest saloon. Never one to condone bullying, Patch had stepped in. The menacing figure in tan buckskins — complete with his trademark eye shade — had soon cowed the startled rannies. They had quickly disappeared to another saloon.

Over a grateful drink, Smollett had poured out his sorry tale. Patch was not slow in weighing up the possibilities that such an addition would make to the gang. Any jasper who was savvy to the working of the banking profession would be a valuable asset. He had not regretted the decision.

And neither had Jim Smollett. Operating on the other side of the counter was far more lucrative, not to say exciting for the ex-bank teller. He had never felt so alive. Unlike Patch and the others, the suave outlaw had a smooth tongue which enabled him to gain the trust and confidence of potential targets. Without these vital particulars, the gang would have been far less successful.

Jack Patch still bossed the gang. He had the nerve and cool detachment necessary when it came to thwarting dangers that lurked around every bend in the trail for guys operating on the wrong side of the law. But Smollett had provided the gang with far more lucrative jobs due to his insider knowledge. It was a good partnership.

The manager of the Express Office

had been more than happy to answer the questions posed by this smartly dressed businessman. And putting one over on arrogant toadies like Abner Bilk was pure icing on the cake.

'We are intending to buy the old Hoskins place next door to expand our enterprise here in Willcox,' Bilk pompously declared, puffing out his chest to impress his slick visitor, not to mention the other clerks as he showed the potential client around. 'The town is situated on an important crossroads and we expect business to boom in the next few years. There are plenty of cattle ranches in the area. And the new silver strike around Tombstone will bring in extra business. Any man who sets up in Willcox will soon make a good profit on his investment.'

Smollett nodded dutifully as the self-important official warbled on, totally unaware of the clandestine reason for the enquiries. His studied gaze took in everything, locking all the relevant details away inside his sharp brain.

'I trust that this vault is solid enough to withstand a determined gang of brigands?' Jim asked carefully, examining the locking mechanism. 'I hear there are some heinous villains operating in Arizona. I'd hate for my funds to be put at risk.'

'Have no fear, sir,' the manager espoused. 'This safe is the latest model. The door is set on a time lock mechanism and constructed of the finest steel that is impossible to blast open. And the inside is lined with two layers of brick. Rest assured, your money will be safe with us.'

'That's all I wanted to hear, Mr Bilk.'

* * *

The Express Office vault backed on to the empty building. An ideal spot from which to break in through the partition wall on Saturday with a full day extra to escape into the wide blue yonder before the raid was discovered the following Monday. And most important of all, there was a strong box inside with at least $30,000 supposedly awaiting transit to the head office at Globe that same day. Three months' takings just waiting for some enterprising men to pick up.

The sartorial outlaw smiled, thinking how easy it was going to be for the gang to lift all that dough and disappear without a trace. And not a shot fired.

'I'm pleased that you are impressed with our operation here, Mr Jones,' the manager preened. 'If you come in on Monday morning, perhaps we can review terms of business to suit us both?'

The two men shook hands. 'I am sure that will be satisfactory, sir,' the bogus entrepreneur murmured in his most urbane voice. 'I will discuss your proposals with my associates over the weekend.'

Back in the hidden draw, a noise had alerted one of the gang who had been on watch. 'There's somebody coming, boss,' a hairless jasper known only as Bonehead called down from a rocky ledge. The whole gang were instantly on their feet, guns drawn just in case. But they soon relaxed as the dark-suited rider trotted into view.

'How'd it go, Jim? Are we in business?' Patch enquired eagerly before the rider had even dismounted.

'It was just like you figured, boss,' Smollett announced, accepting a welcome mug of coffee. 'There's an added bonus as well. A door round back of the empty store gives direct access to the room abutting the Express Office. And it isn't overlooked by any other buildings. We can leave the horses right outside.'

Patch rubbed his hands, an avaricious glint in his one eye all the more poignant. 'If'n we wait until after dark tonight, that should give us plenty of time to break through the wall and lift the dough.' He chuckled uproariously. 'Those jaspers are gonna get the surprise of their lives come Monday.'

He slapped Smollett on the back. 'That sure was a lucky break when I met up with you, buddy.'

Gentleman Jim was not about to disagree with that. 'And one other thing,' he said while forking a lump of fried deer meat into his mouth. 'I managed to persuade a guy with a wagon heading our way to carry the goods for us.' Patch stiffened. The announcement received a sceptical frown of censure. 'Don't worry, Jack,' Smollett hurriedly assured him. 'He was down on his luck and more than eager to help out. His name is Henry Douglas. I offered him $1,000 which he jumped at. And that way, we're in the clear should a posse catch up with us. No loot, no crime.'

Patch scratched his stubbly chin. He was still not convinced. No other gang that he knew of had ever tried something like that before. 'I don't know, Jim. Bringing in some jasper we don't know. How can you be certain we can trust this guy? He could leave us high and dry then light out with the dough.'

'Not a chance. He ain't got the balls.' Self-assurance oozed from Smollett's whole demeanour. 'And he has a wife with him. I laid it on thick as a prime rib steak. Double-cross the Patch Gang and there would be nowhere to hide. That sure put the frighteners on him.' Smollett sat back, puffing confidently on his cigar before adding, 'Haven't I always come good in the past?'

There was no denying that taking on Gentleman Jim had been one of Jack Patch's better ideas. He looked an implausible outlaw, but that didn't matter just so long as he served a useful purpose. And gaining the confidence of jumped-up officials like Abner Bilk had sure paid dividends.

The gang leader smiled. 'You ain't just a handsome dude, Jim. Smart as well. I like it.' He turned to the others. 'Soon as it gets dark, we'll head into Willcox by different routes and all meet up round back of the Express Office.'

★　★　★

Arriving in ones and twos, nobody paid the apparent drifters any attention. Affecting a casual ease, they turned down the narrow alleyway adjacent to the Wells Fargo depot. As promised, the wagon driver paid to transport the expected loot was there waiting.

'You know what to do?' Patch rasped without any greeting. He adopted his most intimidating glare, pinning the anxious guy down with his lone peeper, still not entirely won over with this part of the plan.

'Don't worry, Mr Patch. I'll be in Nogales with the goods as agreed,' the man replied. 'You can count on me.'

'You better be right, fella.' The implied threat hung in the still air. 'Smollett said you had a wife. I don't see her.'

'I didn't want Laura involved. So I left her back at our campsite east of town. Told her I was going in for some extra supplies needed for the journey to Nogales.'

Patch grunted. Just so long as the critter delivered, that was all he was bothered about. 'This job is gonna take the best part of the night. So while you're waiting, make yourself useful in here with us.' A disdainful eye ran across the puny looking jasper. 'You can keep us supplied with vittles.'

He then moved across to examine the back of the abandoned store. And one more piece of good fortune was there to greet him. The door at the rear of the empty building was not even locked. The gang were inside within minutes of arriving. Having done his bit, Jim Smollett was given the job of first watch. Casually patrolling outside, he could give warning to the vault crackers of any potential danger.

'I'll have one of the boys relieve you in two hours. Then it's your turn for a spot of manual labour as well.' Patch smiled. It lacked any warmth, a challenge for the pen-pusher to get his hands dirty like the rest of them.

Smollett met his gaze with one of equal detachment. 'I ain't afraid of hard work if'n that's what you think, Jack.' He spat on his hands. 'Afore joining the bank, I worked on a railroad gang for a spell to earn enough money for a banking course. I can swing a lump hammer as good as anybody here.'

'We'll soon find out, I guess,' muttered the suitably impressed leader.

Picks and crowbars were needed to loosen and dig out the brickwork. Spare clothing had been volunteered by each man to muffle the sound of the heavy work. Even so, in the confined space, the racket sounded like the charge of a rampant herd of buffalo. Within a short time, the room was filled with choking dust. The diggers were forced to tie bandannas over their faces.

'Go outside, Greylag,' Patch ordered soon after they had started. 'Let me know if'n you can hear anything.'

The outlaw reported back that he

could hear the noise but only immediately outside the empty building. That was good news, enabling the breakthrough to go ahead in earnest.

For the work to continue unabated, Patch had arranged a shift system by which each man was given a ten minute break every hour. Luckily the cement bonding was friable and easily chipped out. By early Saturday morning, the first layer of bricks had been removed, producing a hole some five feet in diameter.

'That was a piece of cake, boys,' Patch declared, tipping a large slug of whiskey down his throat. 'If'n the inner lining is anything like that, we'll be in and out of that vault well before first light.'

Unfortunately, this second skin of newer brick proved to be much more resilient. The transit agency must have had the existing wall specially reinforced as extra protection. It was something that had not been foreseen.

Patch cursed aloud. At the rate they

were going, it would be daylight before they broke through. No sense carping on about it now. They would all need to redouble their efforts. Assuming that everybody in town would now be fast asleep, Patch had brought all his forces to bear on a final single-minded push to break through the wall, the outside sentinel included.

Even the wagon driver had been drafted in to assist. Sweat was soon pouring off dirt-smeared faces.

It was around four in the morning when they finally smashed through. Sighs of relief greeted the small hole that appeared. A muted cheer went up. After that, it was much easier to extract the loosened bricks. It was Patch who scrambled through the gap to inspect the inside of the bank vault. He lit a match, holding it up.

Shelves of documents on one side were matched by accounting ledgers on the other. These were of no interest. Bags of coins were also ignored as being too heavy. But there in the middle of the floor stood their objective, the iron bound strong box. A heavy lock prevented access to the contents. No way could it be broken open until they were well clear of the town.

'Give me a hand with this monster, Blackie,' Patch ordered. Being the most burly of the outlaws, Hayes helped him drag the box through the rough-hewn gap.

Once it had been man-handled into the adjacent building, all the men gathered round, staring open-mouthed. Avaricious eyes feasted upon this, their ticket to the good life. Imaginations immediately ran riot. According to Smollett, there was enough dough in there to set them all up on Easy Street for a good long period once they were over the border into Mexico.

So enamoured were the ogling brigands they were almost caught out when a gatecrasher burst into the debris-choked room.

Teddy Blue Flobert, a drunken cowboy, had just woken up and

wandered down the alley to relieve himself. He was singing a tuneless ditty. But the robbers were so mesmerized by their haul they failed to heed the intruder. It was just as well that Teddy Blue was three sheets to the wind. He tripped over his own feet while trying to expose himself and fell against the unlocked door.

'Aaaaagh!' The cry of alarm found him stumbling inside the empty store-room. That was when he received his second surprise.

'What in tarnation are you guys doing in here?' he slurred out, trying to regain his feet. Panic-laden eyes panned across the eight grim faces. It didn't take long for his sluggish brain to figure out that some kind of skulduggery was afoot here. 'Hey! That's a strong box lying there.' A shaking hand then pointed to the hole in the wall. His eyes bulged.

'You guys are robbing the Express Office.' His mouth opened, ready to holler out a warning.

Klute was the first to recover his senses. The hothead grabbed his revolver. Two bullets struck the poor sap in the chest, a third smashing the back window. Flobert didn't stand a chance.

The reverberation bounced off the walls. It had been a reflex action on the part of the young gunslinger. No amount of shouting would have alerted the citizens of Willcox from in the back room. But gunfire was another matter entirely, especially at this early hour in the morning.

'God darn it! That racket will have set the cat among the pigeons. Let's get out of here,' Patch snapped. There was no point in uttering recriminations against the rash deed of his madcap junior. He would have used a knife. But it was too late for such considerations now. 'Hayes and Bonehead. You two shift that box outside on to the wagon.'

The others quickly mounted up while the wagon driver swung his team of four around to head in the opposite direction.

'You know where to meet up?' Patch said. 'Pinecone Draw, two miles west off the Tucson trail.'

'I know it,' the driver replied.

'Well, make sure you show up.' A gimlet eye oozing menace bored into the nervous guy. Patch was exceedingly loath to place their ill-gotten gains into the hands of this milksop. But there was no way they could carry the heavy box away on horseback.

Henry Douglas slapped the leathers, considering it prudent to stifle any adverse retort. He soon disappeared amidst an amalgam of old shacks and back lots.

'OK, boys,' Patch hollered, leaping into the saddle. 'Time we ate dust.'

As the seven riders swung on to the main street, shouts erupted from a myriad of throats. It was patently obvious that the three gunshots from Klute had indeed alerted the town.

'What's going on?' called out one

bystander who had emerged from the general store in his night shirt. 'Who fired those shots at this early hour?'

Another slung a pointing arm towards the fleeing brigands. 'Those jaspers look like they're up to no good,' he shouted, adding to the growing sense of disquiet.

'That's Jack Patch, ain't it?' another startled onlooker declared. 'I recognize him from a wanted dodger on the town notice board. There's a reward of $2,000 out for his capture.' That observation was all that was needed for the gathered citizens to haul off with whatever firearms they had to hand.

Bullets zipped past the heads of the fleeing outlaws. Bent low over the necks of their horses, the robbers strove to avoid the storm of lead. All too soon for the irate citizens, the thieves were out of range. Patch kept up a frantic pace for the next fifteen minutes until they were back in the hidden draw. The horses needed to rest up before they could begin their flight to the border. That was when Greylag spoke up, realizing they were one man down. 'Where's Smollett?' he barked.

Nobody answered. The others looked askance. Surprise more than alarm was written across their hard faces. Then the obvious conclusion was drawn.

'Looks like he bought it,' remarked an apathetic Klute with a shrug. 'All the more dough for us then, boys.'

'Must have been during that wild flurry of shots when we fled Willcox,' commented a hard-nosed villain called Arby Tench. He likewise shrugged off the loss. No regrets were voiced. It was one of the risks they took. And in truth, Gentleman Jim had never really been one of them.

The boss was more concerned about the whereabouts of Henry Douglas. 'That guy better show up or he's dead meat,' he growled.

For the next ten minutes they were all on tenterhooks. The tension in Pinecone Draw was palpable. It was only when the familiar sound of

creaking leather and squeaking axles cut through the heavy silence that the strained atmosphere noticeably eased. The wagon trundled into the clearing with Douglas sitting up on the bench seat.

The glow of a false dawn provided sufficient light to see that he was alone.

They hurried across. Without preamble, Patch jumped into the back of the wagon. Along with Blackie Hayes, the heavy box was pushed out. It landed on the hard-packed earth with a dull thud. Not wishing to create any undue noise, a lump hammer was wielded to smash the lock. A collective intake of breath followed as the seven men stood over the iron-bound box as Jack Patch tentatively raised the lid.

Seven pairs of eyes stared down as the contents were revealed. For a brief moment, silence ensued. But it was momentary. Klute was the first to emit a howl of delight.

'Yeeeehaaaw!!' he sang out. 'Now ain't that a sight for sore eyes.'

There was no denial of that fact from anybody. Piles of lovely greenbacks stacked neatly in the box stared back at the ogling villains. But Patch knew this was no place to celebrate. They were much too close to the robbery scene.

'OK, boys. We need to hit the trail, pronto. Time enough to wallow in our success when we're over the border.' He turned to address Douglas. 'Have you got a safe place to keep that box in case you get stopped?' he asked pointedly.

'There's a special compartment for tools under the front seat of the wagon. We can put the box in there.'

Patch was still sceptical. 'What about that wife of your'n? Won't she kick off knowing her loving husband is transporting stolen goods?'

'I don't intend telling her until you've paid me off,' Douglas said. 'Figured it best that way. What she doesn't know can't hurt her. And it will give me the grubstake I need to set up in the freight hauling business.'

That pledge appeared to satisfy the

distrustful gang boss. 'OK then. You take the easier route through Tombstone and Sierra Vista. The rest of us are heading south through the Santa Rosa Valley. We should all reach Nogales in about ten days' time.'

Soon after that the two factions parted. But ten days is a long time. Much could happen during that period.

2

Desecration

Matthew Devlin was busy writing when the six men burst through the church doors. Afternoon Sunday School for the children was over. There were no more services that day. Following a cup of coffee secretly laced with whiskey and a slice of his wife's cinnamon cake, the rest of the day was his own. At this time, he always liked to sit opposite the cross of Our Lord while trying to gain inspiration for his next sermon.

Nobody in the small Arizona town of Firewall ever called Matt by his Christian name, nor indeed his sur-name. The only exception was his lovely wife, Sarah, who was at that moment preparing the evening meal in the rectory adjoining the church. To his flock it was always Reverend.

Parishioners came from far and wide to pray at the Church of the Good Shepherd, for this was the only permanent building of its kind in the Santa Rosa Valley. It was three months old and had been paid for by public subscription.

The final completion had been readily welcomed by the preacher in preference to the Catalina Saloon on Clovis Street. Now, the good Reverend was able to command the full attention of his flock.

Previously, their gaze had too often strayed to the beer pumps and gambling tables, not to mention the scantily clad female displaying all her charms in garish oil paint above the bar mirror.

The preacher's head lifted from his task at the sudden interruption. He turned around, squinting to discern who had disturbed his thoughts. The men failed to notice the figure sitting on the front row opposite the altar. Their attention was wholly focussed on shaking the rain from grubby yellow slickers and sodden hats. They had ridden steadily south west since leaving the hidden draw near Willcox.

Outside, a howling northerly was battering the small town into submission. This is what had forced these hard-nosed travellers into seeking shelter at the first building they encountered. And that happened to be the church whose doors were always left open, day and night.

'Man, that's one hell of a gale out there,' grunted Greylag. Oldest of the gang, he was a lean-limbed jasper whose grizzled face put his age somewhere between thirty and fifty, depending on whether he bothered to shave. 'Ain't seen the like since that storm over the Mogollons.'

'You ain't kidding there, buddy,' agreed his pal Blackie Hayes, removing a hat to reveal a shock of hair, the colour of which had given him his nickname. 'There's more damn blasted water inside my boots than out there.'

A frown of disapproval crossed the

preacher's face. The thick moustache twitched with irritation. He did not like being disturbed while planning out his sermons. Especially by loud mouth braggarts. This was not the kind of brazen language to be uttered inside God's House. But ever the tolerant man of faith, any impious thoughts were quickly stifled.

He stood up to reveal his full height of six feet plus. Clad in the pastor's uniform of black frock coat and matching necktie, the churchman strolled down the centre aisle.

'Can I be of service to you, gentlemen?' he posed in a firm yet steady voice.

The six men turned as one. Hands routinely dropped to the hoglegs strapped around their hips. Only when they recognized the approaching figure as a man of God did the leader of the group allay their fears.

'It's all right, boys,' he scoffed, intimating the appearance of such a personage was no danger to their presence. 'It's only a Bible basher.' Jack Patch's one good eye ran disdainfully over the Reverend Devlin. But he nonetheless deigned to reply. 'We're sheltering from the weather, preacher boy. You ain't gotten no objections, I trust.'

The pinched look did not expect a rebuttal from the craggy-faced cleric. Nor did he receive one. Matt's face remained impenetrable. 'The Good Shepherd is always open to those who treat his house with respect.' He held the tough jasper's gaze with one of equal frankness. Cause trouble in here and you'll be out that door quicker than forked lightning.

But he kept that thought to himself. The hard fact of one man going up against these hard-bitten critters were poor odds for any successful ejection, even for a man with the backing of Him upstairs.

But Matt Devlin was not fazed. He stood his ground. And waited.

The mounting tension was alleviated

by the sudden appearance of Sarah Devlin at the sacristy door. 'Supper is on the table, Matt — ' The rest of her discourse was cut short on spotting the rough-looking group.

'Well now, what have we here?' drawled Klute.

Ogling peepers leered hungrily at the exquisite profile of the preacher's wife. Even with her hair in disarray and flecked with cornflour, there was no doubting that Sarah Devlin was poetry in motion. That was especially true for a cocky jasper who had only experienced female pleasuring from inside a cat house.

Patch had seen that look numerous times before. And it always spelled trouble where Klute was concerned. The kid's rash temper had proven that assertion in Willcox to the detriment of Jim Smollett. He pushed in front of the young hotshot to suppress any reckless upshot from his subordinate.

'Me and the boys are mighty hungry after our ride, ma'am,' he said, stepping forward into the light cast by a stained glass window. 'We'd be obliged to share your meal, if'n you've a mind.'

It was a thinly veiled order rather than a request. Jack Patch was not a guy to mince his words. The black circle cloaking his dead eyeball lent the gang leader an air of sinister mystique that he played on to the full. The loss was now regarded as a badge of pride. Unfortunately for the perpetrator, he had paid for the honour of its award with his life some two months after the knife fight that caused it.

'Well . . . I don't know . . . ' the woman stammered, unclear what was happening here. 'There's only enough for . . . '

'Then maybe you should rustle up some more, lady,' was the blunt suggestion from the gravel-voiced Bonehead. 'Like the boss said, we're hungry and you seem to have the makings.' The egg-shaped dome jutted forward with intent as he moved down the aisle. The others fell in behind him.

As they passed a table, the sixth man noticed a plate containing a pile of dollar bills. It was the collection from that morning's service. He snatched up the dough. 'This should keep us going for a spell, boys, at least until we all meet up in Nogales.'

Patch reacted with an angry retort. 'Button your lip, Arby,' he hissed, trying to keep his voice low. 'Where we're headed is nobody's business but our own.'

The gaunt hardcase wilted under the restrained harangue. To save face, he grabbed the neck of an adjacent decanter and tipped it to his lips then handed it to Bonehead.

'You can't drink that!' the preacher protested, making to remove the decanter from the offender's grasp. Stolen money was bad enough. But defiling the blessed essence of the Lord's being was sacrilege. 'That's holy wine reserved for those attending communion. You are besmirching the name of God by such a shameful act.'

The two men struggled. At the far end of the church, Sarah yelled out in panic. A nasty situation was rapidly getting out of control. Patch stepped forward. The butt end of his six shooter rose then thudded down on to the exposed head of the preacher. Devlin went down like a sack of potatoes.

Patch's ire was well and truly raised now to fever pitch. 'Somebody grab a hold of the woman while the rest of us get this danged fool tied up to his own cross. He wants to play God, he can hang there and repent of his sins while we fill our bellies.' A well-placed boot sank into the ribs of the unconscious preacher.

In a matter of a few minutes, the earthly world of the Reverend Matthew Devlin had been turned on its head. The gang roughly dragged him up the aisle and strapped his inert form to the wooden cross against the back wall.

'Best gag the critter so he don't raise a ruckus when he finally wakes up,' Patch ordered, standing back to admire his handiwork. 'Now ain't that the best place for the God fearing sonofabitch. All we wanted was some shelter and a bite to eat. And he has to go and spoil things.'

'Matt! Matt!' Sarah cried out, struggling against the encircling arms of Klute who had been quick to obey his leader. Searching hands blatantly caressed the flowing curves of her body. The fact that he was enjoying every second went unheeded. 'Let him down from there, you dirty scum,' she railed impotently. The hopelessly panic-laden riposte was brutally terminated by a backhander from Blackie Hayes. Sarah fell to the floor, blood dribbling from a gashed lip.

'Hey, what you doing, man?' the punk complained. 'I was enjoying that.'

'All that hollering could bring us unwelcome attention,' the tough jasper iterated sharply. 'Ain't you thought of that?'

Klute shrugged. 'Even when she's angry, this gal is still mighty fetching,' he declared, grinning lustfully, the twisted smirk lacking any hint of humour. 'You sure can't deny that, Blackie.'

'I'm more concerned about that grub she's got waiting in the kitchen,' Greylag butted in, slapping the girl's face to bring her round. 'My stomach's growling worse than a wounded puma.'

Sarah stirred, a groan escaping from her blood-caked mouth. Hayes dragged her upright. 'Now you be a good girl and rustle up some chow. And remember, any noise and I'll gag you tight then give you to Klute here for his dessert.'

Howls of laughter greeted this piece of witticism. They came mainly from Klute. 'I sure am looking forward to that, boys. Better than apple pie and cream any day.'

3

Vengeance is Mine . . .

It was around nine o'clock on Tuesday morning when the front door of the church was opened by a grey-haired woman in her middle years. There was a mop and bucket in her hand. Cleaning the church on a Tuesday was Myrtle Safford's first job of the new day.

Monday was the preacher's day of rest. He had stipulated that he was only to be disturbed in an emergency. Even a man of God needed to relax. On this particular week there had been no calls on his spiritual ministrations.

The storm had finally petered out the previous night. Rampant clouds of scudding grey had moved off to the north, attacking the scalloped ramparts of the Galiuro Mountains. From the east, bright sunlight lit up the back wall of the cliff face that surged high above the town. The orange sandstone tableau blazing out in glory had given the town its name. From a distance, the fateful impression of a town in flames had caused many a sharp intake of breath to newcomers. But to locals it was an obvious choice that nobody could dispute on such a fresh morning.

It had been the first rain for over a month. Colourful blossoms took advantage of the life-giving elixir to spread their petals. Steam rose from the wet ground as the sun's heat got to work. Within hours all trace of the cloudburst would be erased as the desert once again claimed the land for its own.

But the blood-curdling scream torn from the cleaner's throat dispelled all thoughts of the weather conditions when she stepped inside the church. The grizzly sight of the Reverend Devlin trussed up on the cross had left her bereft of words for no more than a couple of seconds.

'Help, help!' she yelled out, dashing into the middle of the street. 'The preacher has been attacked and I think he's dead. It's the devil's work. The horned demon is getting his own back on us for building this church. God help us all.' She ran up the street, waving her arms and issuing dire predictions about what had occurred.

'Quieten down, woman!' the mayor snapped, pulling her up short. 'What in tarnation are you burbling on about?'

Myrtle Safford was well known for her gossiping tongue. Others quickly joined him. In minutes she was surrounded by a host of curious citizens. All were eager to learn the cause of her disquieting outburst.

The buxom cleaner took some pacifying before the true horror of what she had witnessed could be dragged out of her. Relating the gruesome details left the poor woman totally distraught. The mayor's wife led her away.

Myrtle was clearly too distressed to re-enter the church. So it was left to

Mayor Elgin, who was also chairman of the Vigilance Committee, to lead the way back to the Good Shepherd.

The pace of the grim procession slowed measurably the closer they drew to the alleged scene of revulsion. Elgin swallowed down a feeling of nausea as he pushed open the door of the church. Fear-laden eyes widened on picking out the silhouette that hung limply at the far end behind the altar. A choking gasp, a lurching of the stomach forced him to stumble back out into the daylight. And there he retched up the contents over the porch railing.

'What is it? What did you see?' asked Doctor Savage, sitting the distraught official down on the steps.

All the mayor could do was point towards the dreadful sight. Tentatively, the men entered the church. Prepared for a grim revelation, under the calming influence of the sawbones, they managed to stave off any unnerving reaction like that which had affected the mayor. Nonetheless, sharp intakes of breath greeted the hideous sight of their preacher hanging there. To a man it felt as if Judgement Day had invaded Firewall in all its rampant fury.

The main body of those present removed their hats and waited nervously at the back of the church while Doctor Savage forced his leaden feet up the aisle to examine the body. His verdict drew gasps of relief from the tense gathering.

'At least he ain't dead,' the medic finally called out. 'Some of you men help me cut him down. He's still badly hurt so we need to be extra careful.'

Lowering the inert figure to the ground, a more thorough assessment revealed that the blood caking the preacher's head was much worse than it looked. The cut on his scalp from Jack Patch's pistol needed bandaging, and there were a few cuts and bruises. He was also suffering from dehydration due to hanging there for so long. Water was dribbled down his throat.

The medic's smelling salts soon

brought life back into the cold frame. Eager hands helped their minister to his feet.

'Stand back, you men,' Savage ordered firmly. 'Give the Reverend some room to breathe.' It was still another ten minutes before Matt was able to stutter out the grim events of the assault.

'Those critters must be long gone by now,' one pertinent observer declared.

Once his mind was working properly, the realization of what had happened hit Matt like a ton of bricks. He peered around. Worried eyes flitted hither and thither, searching every nook and cranny.

'Where's Sarah? Where's my wife?' he cried out. 'She was left at the mercy of those varmints. I dread to think what they've done to her.' He stumbled to his feet. But severely weakened legs gave way and he crashed to the ground. 'Somebody, please. Go find her.' The distraught plea found half a dozen men disappearing into the various alcoves.

41

The others helped him back into a seat. Nobody spoke. What was there to say?

The wait felt like an hour. In effect, it was less than five minutes later when Doctor Savage returned. It was he who had discovered the awful truth. The medic's drawn features left no doubt in anybody's mind as to what he had found. It was agreed by all present that he was the one best suited to deliver the brutal result of the search.

Doctor Savage had to summon all his courage to relate the verdict. 'I'm afraid it ain't good news, Reverend,' he intoned sombrely. 'I-I'm s-orry to tell you that . . . well . . . ' He gulped, unable to continue.

'Just tell me, damn you!' The profane demand was ignored by those present. Who could blame any man, even a preacher, for his profanity under such circumstances? 'I have a God blasted right to know.'

'I'm afraid she didn't make it, Reverend.' A comforting hand rested on the shoulder of the bowed figure. 'And that ain't the worst of it.' He paused, imploring eyes flicking towards the wooden cross, hoping for some form of enlightenment. There was none. A deathly silence filled the void.

Matt Devlin's angst-riddled face turned, willing the medic to finish.

'Her body was . . . violated.'

The hand of Death laid its icy fingers on Matt's heart. He struggled to his feet. A look of anguish imbued his limbs with unaccustomed strength as he pushed aside the gathering. 'Let me through,' he croaked, barely above a whisper. A stumbling gait saw him disappear from view.

Some of the men started to follow, but Doctor Savage held them back. 'This is something he needs to handle on his own.'

It came all too soon. A keening howl like that from a wounded coyote rent the static air. Moments later, the Reverend Matt Devlin emerged from the sacristy carrying the body of his dead wife. Ignoring those present, he staggered down the aisle and outside. The whole town was there to watch as he carried his beloved Sarah down the middle of the street. Complete silence wrapped the town in a shroud of grief. Firewall was in mourning.

* * *

The next few days passed in a haze of mist for Matt. The funeral, the burial in the small cemetery, the meaningless yet sincere tokens of sympathy. All went over his head. He was barely functioning, and then only like a machine. Afterwards when he was sitting in the small kitchen drinking a cup of coffee made by Myrtle Safford, he could barely recall any of it.

All he could remember was seeing the besmirched body of his wife splayed out across the floor. That same floor to which he was now staring. That was when a seething anger suffused his cheeks. Rage burned deep inside his very soul. He grabbed hold of a bottle of whiskey and tipped a liberal slug into his coffee cup. The contents disappeared down his throat in one gulp.

The cleaner gasped, holding her breath. The sudden change in her employer's manner was tangible. Never before had she seen the minister resort to strong drink. She stepped back, fearful of his response to her presence.

But Matt's thoughts were being channelled down a narrow groove. He stood up and went into the church, prostrating himself before the cross. Arms flung wide, he called out loudly on the Lord to reveal himself.

'Why have you, the God of eternal love and salvation, permitted such a brutal act to defile this your most humble servant?'

The answer did not come immediately. But when it did, the words from Romans Verse 12 impinged themselves on to his distraught brain. 'Vengeance is mine, I will repay, saith the Lord!'

Matt breathed deep before adding his own corollary to the biblical quotation which he now voiced in a flat monotone. This was not what he wanted to hear. His head shook in dissent.

'Not this time, Lord. As your ordained representative here on earth, I the Reverend Matthew Devlin, do hereby claim the right to obtain justice for this outrage.' His hand fondled the cross around his neck. His faith was still strong, undiminished. But it had shifted in emphasis. 'Absolution can only be gained through my hands.'

'An eye for an eye, a tooth for a tooth.' The Old Testament quotation from Exodus 21 called out its vengeful message. The wronged man repeated it aloud and with vigour. Mercy and compassion would have to take a back seat. Matt Devlin knew what had to be done.

A fresh resolve suffused features previously blotched with grief. A firm step took the preacher back into the rectory and upstairs to what had been their bedroom. The items he sought were hidden away at the rear of the closet. A suitcase was removed and gingerly opened to reveal a past life. One he thought had been put firmly behind him, but was now about to be resurrected.

And there it lay. Unseen and unused these past two years since Iron Matt Devlin, hired gunfighter and bounty hunter, had given up that life for the cloth. Hands that had carelessly tossed the nickel-plated Colt .45 and its shell belt into the case on that final day now caressed the tooled leather as if it were a delicate flower.

Matt's thoughts flashed back to that last job, the one that had turned him against the life he had chosen and so successfully promoted. It could have been yesterday. In fact it was two years almost to the day. The memory of that grim event would always haunt his dreams. Meeting Sarah Bracknell had saved him from the nightmares that even now still occasionally found him waking up in a cold sweat.

4

Bounty Hunter

The town was called Purgatory. It was located in the Texas Panhandle universally referred to as 'No Man's Land'. With no official control being administered by any legislative body, the narrow strip between Indian Territory and New Mexico had become a magnet for criminal gangs seeking a safe haven from the law. No authorized law enforcement officer would enter the territory. Some had tried in the early days. But nothing more had been heard from them. They had simply disappeared.

According to information supplied by the sheriff of Cimarron, the man Matt Devlin sought was headed east for the Panhandle. Pecos Bob Shadley was wanted across three territories for murder and robbery. He was regarded as a real mean cuss who was not averse to using women and children as shields if cornered. The wanted dodger put out on the brigand made for grim reading. Bringing in this jasper would be a pleasure. The reward on offer was always welcome, but Pecos Bob was someone who needed to feel the rough caress of a hemp rope around his neck.

Matt was no saint himself. But he did have scruples. He only hired out to folks who needed a wrong to be righted. Those incidents which the legitimate agencies were unable, or unwilling to handle. Such deviances had often taken the form of bribes and hand-outs to secure fake alibis in order that the guilty parties could escape their just desserts.

Another 'legitimate crime' that turned Matt's stomach involved pompous money lenders who were able to call in their high interest loans on the flimsiest of pretexts to take control of land, often then sold on for huge profits to railroad companies. Matt had especially relished forcing these charlatans to burn the dubious title deeds before the eyes of their victims. Under such circumstances, his fee was always extracted from the bank accounts of the perpetrators.

Shadley was a regular villain who had thus far evaded all efforts at capture. Heading for the Panhandle ensured that he would not be pursued by any official lawman. As an independent bounty hunter responsible to nobody but himself, Matt Devlin was confident that he was the man to succeed where others had failed.

Even before he crested the rise leading down into Purgatory, Matt's acute hearing picked up the noise emanating from the 'no holds' burg. The place was purely in existence to offer sanctuary and entertainment to itinerant rogues and drifters. The newcomer pulled his hat down and nudged the sorrel along the single main street. It was a reflex action in case there were those around who might recognize the weathered features.

Music and raucous hallooing issued from the numerous drinking parlours. Up above on the veranda of the appropriately named Red Garter saloon, a couple of calico queens called out to the tall stranger. What they had to offer was flagrantly displayed with no hint to the imagination. Matt lifted a languid hand in acknowledgment but carried on.

Nobody else paid any heed to the lone rider. Just another piece of flotsam drifting on the seedy tide of lawlessness. Who else would wish to visit such a place? Permanent residents did live here. But they were mostly Mexicans who carried out the menial tasks that all settlements require to keep them operating. The mean adobe huts on the outskirts of the town clearly provided their habitation.

Matt didn't stop until he was beyond the eastern limits where a lone Joshua tree marked the break of trail. Checking out the lie of the land was a routine he always adopted when entering a strange town. It gave him the edge should a quick getaway be required. Satisfied with the reconnaissance, he swung the horse around, pulling in to one side of the street where he dismounted.

His hawkish gaze flicked about, searching for his quarry. According to the dodger description, Pecos should be easy to eyeball. Apparently he always wore an eagle feather in his grey Stetson, together with a watch and chain secured to his vest. This latter had been stolen from the man who had secured Matt's services. His only daughter had been killed by Shadley during a stagecoach robbery near Raton Pass.

But what caught Matt's attention was the saddle atop a paint mare tied outside Saucy Sue's Pleasure Palace. The artistic depictions advertising what was on offer inside were garish and bawdy as befitted such an establishment in a place like Purgatory where the vast majority of visitors were male.

An appreciative hand traced a path over the smooth brown leather of the Porter double cinched saddle, model number seventy-eight favoured by Texans. At least Bob Shadley had good taste in horse tack. This distinctive item indicated the mount likely belonged to his mark. The Texas desperado appeared to have opted for some frisky pecker-popping before lunch. A crafty smile from his pursuer stared down at the crumpled reward poster on which he now boldly wrote a message in blue crayon.

It read: *East end of town by the Joshua Tree. Be there in ten minutes.*

Prior to entering the Palace, he made certain of his escape route down a back alley behind the building where he tethered his horse. As expected, a rear door on the second floor gave on to a flight of steps. Fire was a constant hazard in towns primarily constructed of wood. Such measures were accordingly deemed essential.

Back out front, he stepped inside the

lascivious establishment where a veri-
table array of aromas assailed his
nostrils, each designed to entice the
client to linger. Girls in various states of
undress lay sprawled on cushioned
divans, adopting what were meant to be
alluring poses. They came in all ages,
offering falsely enticing smiles. Matt
had never felt the need to make use of
such premises. And the lack-lustre
display of feminine flotsam on offer
here did nothing to alter his stance.

'Can I help you, sir?' The purred
enquiry came from a woman old
enough to be his mother. Could this be
the ubiquitous Saucy Sue? Clearly she
was not one of the ladies for hire. And
he could readily see why.

Matt launched into the spiel he had
prepared before entering this den of
iniquity. 'I'm here to join my buddy. He
availed himself of your services earlier
in the day. But he ain't expecting me
until tomorrow. We agreed that I should
join him on a two-some when I arrived.'
Matt ignored the madam's puzzled

look. 'Reckoned he was gonna pay double for the privilege.'

Sue shook her head of frizzy blond curls. 'I know nothing about this. Who is this guy? Cos he sure ain't paid any extra.'

'You'd know him on account of a gold watch chain and the feather in his hat.'

That piece of information certainly struck home. 'Ah, you must be referring to Mr Smith. But if'n you want to join him it will cost you an extra ten dollars.'

'And cheap at the price, madam,' warbled Iron Matt, laying down the required fee.

'He's on the first floor in room number six,' Sue replied with a knowing wink. 'And if'n Bella don't suit your needs, handsome, I'm sure we can fix you up with somebody more alluring.' She wiggled her ample hips while thrusting a bosom akin to a couple of ripe melons in his face.

Matt smiled back. 'I might well take you up on that, ma'am,' he casually intoned. 'Number six, you say. My buddy is gonna be in for a big surprise.' He didn't elucidate what that would entail. But it was likely to shake the Palace to its foundations. Access to the upper storey sported a lurid sign painted in gold — *Stairway to Heaven*. Matt couldn't resist a murky aside, 'Hell in your case, Mr Smith.'

'What was that, sir?' enquired Saucy Sue.

'Just talking to myself, is all,' came back the casual reply as Matt cat-footed up the velvet draped stairs. Room six was at the end. Various indications of other patrons enjoying the goods on offer could be heard through the closed doors as he passed by. Beyond number six, a door gave access to the rear of the premises. A quick check revealed it was open with access to the back steps. All was going according to plan as the poster was removed from his coat. Quietly, he pushed it under the door and knocked firmly.

No reply. Another louder knock

followed, supplied by the butt end of his gun.

'Get lost, I'm busy,' was the irked retort from inside the room.

'Important message for Mr Smith,' Matt warbled in a high-pitched effeminate voice. The coquettish delivery was followed by a further rap on the door.

Grunts of irritation followed. Creaking springs indicated that Pecos Bob was getting out of bed. Moments later, a sharp croak signified the brigand's alarm as wide eyes took in the full import of the so-called 'message'. The howl of anger that followed was accompanied by three shots. Bullets ripped through the thin wood of the door at chest height. Anybody standing behind it would have been despatched to a hereafter not promised by Saucy Sue.

Moments later, the door was flung open. The shooter rushed out, wearing nought but his hat, a palmed gun at the ready. But the corridor was empty. Like a dream in the night, the courier had vanished, knowing what would be the result of his sly delivery. With the recipient well and truly acquainted with his challenge, Matt quickly departed for the expected rendezvous.

And it was not to be that outlined in blue on the dodger. Experience had taught the bounty hunter how to read the devious mind of his adversary.

Pecos would be figuring out how to avoid any potential showdown in which he might well end up as the filling in a lead sandwich. That would mean heading in the opposite direction on the far side of Purgatory from the Joshua Tree.

Never before had the owlhoot vacated a pleasure dome like Saucy Sue's so quickly. A quick glance down the main street to ensure that no suspicious characters were in sight, he mounted up, swinging the paint mare towards the west.

The crafty smirk behove a notion that he had outflanked his opponent. 'Ain't no damned bounty man gonna get the better of Pecos Bob Shadley,' he muttered into the ears of his cayuse. 'That critter will be waiting 'til doomsday before he gets his own message that this is one sharp dude who won't be adding to his bank balance.'

It was a few moments later when the killer received the shock of his life. Cockahoop that he had outwitted his foe, and passing through the huddle of adobe tenements, a bullet suddenly tore the hat from his head.

The terrified paint reared up on its hind legs, throwing its rider into the dust. Momentarily stunned by the unexpected reversal in his fortunes, the brigand floundered. His turgid brain was desperately trying to figure out what had happened.

A voice laced with acrid hostility punched out from the roof of an abandoned hovel, giving him no chance to retaliate. 'Stay right where you are, scumbag. One false move and you're dog meat.' Another well-placed bullet chewed the leather from Shadley's left boot heel. 'Now stand up slow and shuck that gun belt.'

Matt also stood up, revealing himself. Sundry residents of the Mexican enclave had emerged from their homes. Matt ignored them. Rifle at the ready, he gingerly climbed down a ladder to ground level. One false step could be his last. That was the moment Shadley came back to life.

'No half-baked gunslick is taking me in,' he espoused gruffly. He was well aware as to what awaited him in a court of law. His hand dropped to the holstered Cooper double-action .36. And he was fast, no doubt about it. The gun cleared leather and rose, ready to deliver its lethal charge.

Matt was halfway down the ladder. A vulnerable position in which to be caught. He threw himself off to one side as a bullet from the five-shot Cooper clipped his arm. Rolling over a couple of turns in the dust, he brought the Henry repeater into action.

That was the moment he also received a brutal shock to his system. Far from being abandoned, it appeared that the adobe shack was home to a gang of orphaned kids. One now ran outside to see what was happening. Matt's second shot took the boy in the chest. He was dead before his scrawny frame hit the ground. This awful climax to his grand plan turned the gunfighter's body to ice. What had he done?

It was fortunate indeed that the third of the rapid-fire shots had driven into Bob Shadley's exposed body. It was this last one that did it for the fugitive. Blood spurted from his stomach. Matt waited, spread-eagled on the ground, unable to move. Two human beings dead within the space of two seconds. For Bob Shadley, he harboured no regrets. But a young boy. That was beyond absolution. He buried his head in the hot sand. Tears welled, dribbling into the sand.

Yet still his professional calling, and the will to survive, forced him to check that Shadley posed no further threat. Slowly he rose to his feet. Neither of the two bodies moved. That had been a close call. First he walked over to the blood-stained body of the desperado. Shadley's eyes flickered open. He was still very much alive. The bullet had buried itself in the outlaw's fleshy gut. Although badly wounded, Pecos was not yet ready for a job in the Devil's Kitchen.

He struggled on to one elbow. 'Who . . . are . . . you, mister? I ain't never . . . been . . . caught like that . . . afore.' There was no hint of any remorse for the boy of whose death he had been an integral part. His hand slid towards the fallen Cooper. Matt saw the sly manoeuvre and quickly booted Shadley's pistol aside.

A look of intense loathing coupled with guilt suffused the dark playground of the bounty man's face. Inside, his entrails were twisting into a tight knot of pain. The fact that the kid hailed from Mexican origin was of no consequence. He had snuffed out an innocent life.

With the greatest effort, he strove to contain a burning desire to lash out and destroy the cause of his anguish. But there was no going back. Old Nick's hand was on his shoulder. Mercy was now a dirty word.

'You want to know who I am, Pecos? Then I'll tell you.' A brutish grin scarred the normally handsome visage. 'I'm the Angel of Death come to have his revenge,' he hissed. 'I would have taken you in alive to stand trial. But that option went out the window when you forced me into killing that kid. For that there is no reprieve.' He raised the Colt Peacemaker and rocked back the hammer to full cock.

'Noooooooooo! You can't — !' The horror-stricken howl of lament was cut short as the gun blasted out its terminal farewell.

Once the grim deed had been carried out, Matt picked up the body of the fallen youngster and carried it down to the undertakers.

The boy's compadres followed at a distance. They were muttering and hurling inscrutable insults at the killer of their pal. Matt could not blame them for that.

Only when they began throwing stones and one struck him on the head did he feel the need to retaliate. Swinging round on his boot heel, a rabid growl soon dispersed the irate pack who had no wish to join their dead associate.

Once inside the austere premises of the coffin maker, he slapped a twenty dollar bill on the counter.

'This ought to give the kid more attention than he ever had in life.' A gimlet eye was fixed on to the little weasel in black. 'Make sure he receives a fitting send off. Short change him and I'll hear about it. You get my drift?'

'Sure thing, mister.' The gaunt corpseman nodded vigorously. 'Only the best for young Pedro.' He hesitated before asking about Pecos Bob.

'He's going with me,' Matt replied. 'I still have a living to make. And this jigger is worth just as much dead as alive.'

Ten minutes later, Iron Matt Devlin was back on the trail, retracing his outward journey back to Cimarron. A dozen or so desperadoes had come out of the saloons to see what all the shooting was about. None tried to relieve the hard-bitten bounty hunter of his potential reward. Any jasper who could take down Pecos Bob Shadley deserved the greatest respect. With a six-shooter in one hand and a repeating rifle in the other, Matt was taking no chances.

He cleared the limits of Purgatory with only a lone hound dog for company. And that soon disappeared, chasing after a rabbit.

There was much to think on for the guilt-stricken bounty hunter as he headed west across the Panhandle. Shooting down that kid had shaken him to the core. Life in the guise of a gunfighting vigilante no longer held the exciting challenge it once had. He had always harboured a great respect for the Good Book and its teachings. On the second night out, he had a dream, more like a vision, where an angel appeared pointing the way forward. By the time he awoke the next morning, Iron Matt Devlin knew in which direction his future lay.

A Bible would take the place of the Colt. No longer would peacemaking be accompanied by a gun. The iron hand would now wear a soft kid glove. Forgiveness rather than revenge would be his maxim.

5

Cast Afoot

Matt Devlin, self-appointed harbinger of justice, slung the leather gun belt around his trim waste and fastened up the heavy brass buckle. After tying the thong around his right thigh, he settled the rig comfortably. It had been a long time. Yet the tool of his old trade felt like it was still part of him.

A momentary pang of doubt crossed his jumbled mind. Was he doing the right thing? Yet again, a hand strayed to the wooden cross around his neck. Touching the sign of his faith gave him confidence, but no answer to his quandary. If he reverted to gun law, could he ever return to the life he had so earnestly followed without the support of his beloved Sarah?

Matt sank to his knees. Head bowed,

he once again prayed fervently for divine support that what he was about to embark upon was justified. The answer was long in coming, and conjured up by a man distraught with grief. Spiritual direction, such as it was, would be made to fit the dire circumstances into which he had been thrust. And once acknowledged, there would be no going back.

With the dilemma finally resolved and his mind made up, Matt felt like a new man. His ministerial regalia was discarded in favour of the range gear normally reserved solely for when he went hunting in the hills behind Firewall. He would now be hunting down men — and not for the purpose of saving their souls. The burning flames of Hell Fire were the only place for such sinners.

From that moment he was like a man possessed. The sooner he departed on his mission the better. A wire was sent to Pastor Chadwick Varney, an itinerant cleric who visited remote settlements throughout southern Arizona where pious succour was in short supply. Varney was based in Tucson and would doubtless welcome the chance of ministering to a permanent flock. Matt's fervent hope was for it to be a temporary basis only.

That was the plan. Although, Matt was under no illusions that his task of divine retribution would be simple to accomplish.

A reply to his cable was received the following day with a positive response from Varney. It was invariably tinged with regret at the dire circumstances of his appointment.

Matt wasted no time in packing his saddle-bags. Following a muted farewell to Doctor Savage over a substantial breakfast prepared by Myrtle Safford the next morning, he was ready to head out into the unknown.

'You'll need a good lining on your stomach, Reverend, where you're headed,' the old woman guardedly advised. She then handed him a package for the journey. 'This should keep the wolf from the door for a spell. And may God go with you.'

Matt thanked her, his eyes lifting towards the Heavens. 'We'll have to see about that, eh, boss?' he muttered under his breath, hand resting on the bone handle of his trusty Colt.

His eye caught that of the doubtful sawbones. Savage had tried unsuccessfully to persuade the stubborn pastor of the need to let the official law deal with the matter.

'Arizona is a big territory, Doc,' Matt iterated with a shake of the head. 'Too darned big for a handful of lawmen to cover. And until such time as every town has its own marshal, wronged guys like me have to bite the bullet by cleaning up our own mess.' A caustic frown silenced the expected rejoinder. 'And that's an end of it. No more arguments.'

He stood up and went outside where his faithful sorrel was waiting patiently. Myrtle and the doctor followed. There was no more to be said. But that didn't stop worried looks cloaking their restrained good wishes for a successful outcome to their minister's vendetta. Or was it a holy crusade?

Iron Matt left the rectory by way of a back trail. The last thing he needed was having to acknowledge the well-meaning platitudes of his flock. Facing those people who were friends as well as parishioners would be heart-rending and liable to temper his resolve. Something he could well do without.

All too soon, the town of Firewall disappeared from view as he entered the dense covering of pine forest behind. Would he ever see the town again? It didn't bear thinking on. So he brushed the depressing notion aside.

An hour later, he rejoined the main trail heading south. His destination was the Mexican town of Nogales. It was a good ten days' steady riding so there was no time to lose if he was to catch up with the killers before they crossed the border. Matt was prepared to go anywhere to hunt down the rats. But Mexico was an unknown quantity with a volatile government that he was loath to provoke with gunplay. Far better to net his quarry on the American side where the law was more likely to empathize with his quest.

* * *

It was on the second day out of Firewall when trouble struck, albeit from an unexpected quarter.

He was attacked by a band of Mescalero Apaches. The first he knew of their presence was an arrow buried deep in his horse's neck. Another lethal barb missed his leg by a hair's breadth quivering in the saddle horn. But the animal was done for. It staggered on for a few more faltering steps before collapsing in a heap of thrashing limbs.

Matt threw himself off to the left, then quickly scrambled behind the inert bulk for cover.

It was lucky for him that the band

comprised only six braves who possessed no firearms. A couple of shots despatched their way soon made them realize that bows and arrows were no match for a Winchester repeater.

A stand-off ensued. The Indians were concealed in a cluster of rocks while their intended victim huddled behind his dead cayuse. Sooner or later, Matt knew that they would surround him. He didn't have eyes in the back of his head. So even with a Winchester, that would surely be the end of his quest before it had started. There had to be a way out of this dangerous situation.

Matt surmised that they must be a hunting party. Yet a glance at their own stringy horseflesh led him to the conclusion that their trip had not been a success. No carcases of deer, rabbit or other eatable creatures graced their mounts.

An hour passed with no movement from either faction. Something had to give soon. Even now they could be creeping into position to finish him off.

Perhaps these jaspers only wanted food. And his horse would provide many meals for hungry mouths. He fondly patted the still warm carcase.

'We've been together a good few years,' he murmured. 'Pity it has to end this way, old gal. But I reckon you'd understand.'

He then decided to test the theory, calling out in sonorous voice, 'Do you of the Mescalero tribe seek food for your lodges?'

Like an eagle on the wing, the terse enquiry carried across the stark landscape to where the Indians were concealed. And it had clearly been heeded. A head wrapped in a grubby red bandana poked above a boulder. 'It is as you say, white eye,' the brave called back. 'Our women and children will die soon without meat.'

'Let me go and my horse is your'n for the taking,' was the brisk reply. Matt held his breath while the spokesman for the group consulted his men.

After what seemed like an eternity,

the stilted monotone of the Mescalero red cap allowed the concealed man to breathe easy. 'We do not seek your hide, white eye, only your horse. Go now and do not look back. Next time we meet, the gods may not be so generous.'

Matt was well aware of what that intimated. A hand automatically lifted to his scalp. Slowly he stood up, gripping the stock of the rifle but making certain to keep it lowered.

Sharp eyes were fixed firmly on the rocks as he backed off. Just in case these red devils decided that the addition of human meat would make for a more triumphant hunting expedition.

The six Indians stood up. Silhouetted across the azure backdrop, unmoving, the bleakly austere figures appeared to have been sculpted from the hard desert sandstone of which they were a part. Matt quickened his step. He would not feel safe until well clear of the killing ground. His breathing eased when the Apaches moved down to their deceased prize and began cutting it up.

Cast afoot, he turned about heading south towards the scalloped ridgeback of the Dragoon Mountains. At least he had his side-arm and rifle so he would not starve out here in the wilderness, a sandy wasteland known as the Madera Sink. Ten miles did not seem a long way. But having to trudge that sort of distance on foot soon began to tell. Riding boots were only designed for the shortest of walks. Matt's pace noticeably slowed as the hours passed.

He was also wondering where he could secure another mount.

And then it began to rain. The first hint of a flash storm that could blow up at any time were heavy droplets thudding on to the wide brim of his hat. He groaned. His waterproof slicker had been left behind. Within minutes he was soaked to the skin. Visibility was reduced to his immediate surroundings. Yet still he trudged onward, head down and trusting to providence that he was going in the right direction.

Time ceased to have any significance. One sore foot followed the other as he plodded forwards. Shadows were caressing the harsh landscape as he stumbled into a tree-choked gulch which offered some respite from the incessant downpour. He paused beneath the shelter of a rocky overhang. Night was announcing its arrival when he noticed a glimmer of light up ahead. It looked like a campfire.

But friend or foe? That was the question. After ten miles of foot slogging, he was in desperate need of shelter and sustenance. Being stuck out in the open overnight held no appeal whatsoever. There was only one way forward.

It was fortunate this was the month of July and not December or the dousing would have finished him off long before this. As it was, he needed a moment within the temporary refuge of the overhang to gather himself for the affray, if such the forthcoming encounter proved to be. The earnest expectation was that these were indeed his wife's killers.

Now that a showdown was imminent, Matt fervently hoped that his revolver would live up to Sam Colt's assertion that rainfall had no effect on the gun's firepower. The cartridges were enclosed in sealed brass casings allegedly immune to the wet. And so was the Winchester. A couple of years back when cap and ball action was standard, this would not have been the case.

Should these jaspers be part of the Patch Gang, the next few minutes would decide the matter once and for all. There would be no taking of prisoners should they decide to resist. A showdown was most definitely his preferred choice.

He looked to the bubbling grey of the Heavens and despatched a plea of understanding. His hand gently caressed the wooden cross concealed beneath his wet shirt.

With devout succour gained, he then

laid a hand on more immediate help — the butt of his revolver. Since leaving Firewall so abruptly, Matt had ably proved to himself that his prowess in the deadly art of triggernometry had not suffered. So he was confident of being able to deal with any resistance.

But it was not without some trepidation that he moved forward gingerly. Unlike many of his gun-slinging contemporaries, killing did not come easily to the ex-bounty hunter. Why else had he forsaken the path of violence to take up the Good Book? And once his present quest had been fulfilled, Matt Devlin passionately hoped that he would once again be capable of resuming his service to the Lord.

But first there was more earthly work to accomplish. Two tethered horses emerged from the rain-charged murki-ness. Voices could be heard coming from inside a cave. He moved forward, deliberately cracking a dead branch to alert those sheltering inside to his presence. The talking stopped abruptly.

'Whoever's out there, show yourself, pronto, if'n you don't want a load of buckshot heading your way.'

Matt tensed. He would recognize that lazy southern drawl until his dying day. It hailed from the critter whom the gang leader had called Arby. The one he had tackled before being laid out cold with a gun butt. Carefully moving into the open, he raised his hands to give the impression he meant them no harm. Immediately he saw that his supposition was correct. Never in a bunch of lifetimes would he forget that skeletal visage. His buddy was the bald galoot who had been more interested in filling his belly. Both men had risen and were hunched down, ready for trouble.

As expected, the two men did not recognize the newcomer. Matt was well aware that most folks only perceived what their senses told them. A guy wearing range duds and a wide brimmed Stetson was definitely no preacher. Shaving off his moustache had also substantially altered his appearance. Only the most observant person would have expected otherwise. These jaspers were certainly not that sharp.

'I'd be obliged for some of that coffee,' Matt innocently enquired, effecting a hangdog look. 'It's mighty wet on the trail. Especially for a guy cast afoot.'

'You alone, mister?' Bonehead asked, trying to pierce the opaque gloom behind this unwelcome intruder.

Matt nodded, stepping forward. 'I've been walking for the last ten miles. Coming across you guys sure was a stroke of luck.' No hint was proffered as to the true meaning of that remark.

'Luck, you say? There's good and bad. A guy makes his own, I'd say. Maybe luck brought you this way. Then again . . . maybe not.' This from Arby Tench whose suspicious nature had not been assuaged by the newcomer's innocuous disposition. 'And stay right where you are until we're satisfied you're on the level.'

'So what happened to your horse?' asked Bonehead.

Matt offered a nonchalant lift of the shoulders. 'I'm just a lonesome traveller like yourselves. All I ask is to share your fire and maybe a bite to eat. Ain't nothing wrong with that, is there?'

'Just answer the question, fella,' Bonehead rasped, waving the shotgun menacingly. 'Like my pard said, we don't trust nobody who drifts in here uninvited.'

'Some Mescalero bucks attacked me down the trail apiece. Stuck an arrow head in my horse's neck. It was my good fortune they were only after the meat. Guess they were as hungry as I am now.'

'What do you reckon, Arby?'

The hardcase shrugged. 'Guess it's all right. OK, help yourself, mister. The coffee's hot and strong but there ain't no cream or sugar.'

'Just as I like it,' Matt intoned,

accepting the proffered mug, genuinely grateful for the warmth it provided.

He sat down opposite the two campers on the far side of the flickering blaze. Bonehead handed him a plate after ladling out some beans into which were embedded chunks of fatback. It looked revolting, but beggars can't be choosers and Matt quickly shovelled it down. 'Boy, I sure needed that,' he said, licking the grease from his lips. And he meant it.

The two desperadoes eyed the stranger in their midst. Silence engulfed the cave as capering shadows danced across the rough-hewn walls.

'So where you headed?' Tench finally asked, filling his own mug with coffee.

Matt paused before answering. Adopting a mellow satisfaction provided by the food, he casually replied, 'South west of here to Nogales. There's some business that needs clearing up down there.'

The two men visibly stiffened.

'And what business might that be?'

Bonehead growled. His hand surreptitiously fell to the gun on his hip. Matt was not slow in noting the move. But his hard face gave nothing away. 'Must be mighty important to bring a fella out on a day like this.'

'You could say that,' Matt replied in a low murmur. 'Fact is, I'm tracking some bad boys who done me a deal of harm.' A steely regard fastened on to the two men. He pulled out the makings from his pocket and casually rolled a stogie before adding, 'You wouldn't by any chance have come across a gang of skunks led by a dude wearing a black patch?'

The two men cast worried looks at each other. 'How many in this gang?' Bonehead croaked out.

'I counted six. And it looks like I've come across two of them already.' He reached into his shirt and hooked out the wooden cross. 'Recognize this, do you?' A pair of disbelieving peepers stared at the carved image. 'Reckon I don't need to ask that. Seeing as you've already seen it back in Firewall.'

'It's that damned preacher!' The startled exclamation hissed out from beneath Arby Tench's bushy moustache. 'God Almighty!'

'You rats figure He's gonna help you?' Matt spat, lurching to his feet. 'I doubt it. But let's find out. Now grab your hardware. It's time for the Good Lord to decide who's side he's on.'

In the blink of an eye, the two brigands were reaching for their revolvers. The twilight world of the remote cave was suddenly lit up by flashes of gunpowder. The air reverberated under the crash of exploding shells. Upwards of ten shots must have been fired off in less than that equivalent in seconds. A series of panic-laden squawks heralded the sudden flight of roosting quails that had also taken refuge during the storm. They were followed by a scampering pair of rabbits.

When the smoke dispersed, Matt Devlin was standing over the bodies of Arby Tench and his pal known as

Bonehead. Both men had discovered the hard way that the Lord had indeed decided they were the guilty parties. Their passport to the paradise of the afterlife had been refused. They were now in the hands of Old Nick and his minions.

A silence all the more poignant settled over the grim scene of devastation. Matt clutched the wooden cross to his chest, murmuring under his breath as another quotation, this time from Genesis, impinged itself on his thoughts — 'Whosoever kills Cain, vengeance will take him sevenfold.'

A cynical smile forced apart the tightly clenched mouth. 'Six in this case. Two of the bastards down, four to go.' His eyes lifted to the rough ceiling of the cave. 'And if'n that means I lose your forgiveness, Lord, then so be it. This is one time when showing the other cheek is going to be laid aside.' No hint of remorse for his death-dealing actions showed on the craggy façade. Nothing, neither in Heaven nor on Earth, was going to sway the resurrected bounty hunter from his mission of retribution.

This was only the start. Then he held the cross out over the unmoving corpses. 'And may the Lord turn his back on your miserable souls. Where you boys are headed, there will be no angels strumming on harps.'

The blood-stained cadavers were removed from the cave. They would provide a surprise feast for any passing scavengers.

Matt then stripped off his sodden garments and set them by the fire to dry out. More dry wood was heaped on the dying embers. Commandeering one of the bedrolls, he laid it out and settled down for the night. For the first time since that ghastly discovery at the Good Shepherd, he slept right through, his slumbers undisturbed by any nightmares.

6

Mission of Doom

Matt was up early the next morning. He didn't need to look outside the cave to see that the storm had passed.

Not to mention the two bodies which had been removed. Only a few shreds of clothing were left to mark the presence of Arby Tench and Bonehead on this earth. 'And good riddance,' muttered the pitiless avenger, his gaze cool as the creek water flowing through the narrow gulch. 'At least you fellas gave some hungry creatures a decent meal.'

White bolls of fluffy cloud sidled across a blue backdrop. Beams of welcome sunlight lanced across the floor. And best of all, his clothes had dried out. Taking full advantage of the makings bequeathed by the dead owlhooters, Matt cooked himself a decent breakfast of bacon and beans washed down with fresh coffee. He cleaned up in the creek overflowing with the previous night's rain, then packed away the inherited trail pack.

Two horses stood patiently waiting close by. Both needed feeding. The finest of the pair was an appaloosa which he saddled up. The other, a raggy mustang he tethered with an extended rein before leading it off back down the gulch. The tortuous trail slithering around knots of rough-hewn sandstone eventually brought him out on to the open plain south of the Dragoons. He was then able to nudge the horses to a steady canter.

And with the golden glow of the new day's sun rising splendidly on his left, Matt set a course for the distant upthrust of the Tumacácori Range, beyond which lay his objective. Scrub vegetation comprising dwarf oak and juniper was interspersed with stands of towering Saguaro cactus plants. There was no trail but it was clear that some riders had passed this way within the last few days.

And judging by the number of hoof prints, they had to be those of the Patch Gang. After a half hour, the trail split. One set of prints branched left. The others clearly etched in the previous day's damp sand pointed to the south west. And there were three of them.

This confirmed that the varmints were indeed heading for Nogales. It also indicated that the gang had taken the precaution of separating for safety reasons.

Patch was clearly no fool. The border town was a stone's throw from the border. The gang boss must indeed harbour the intention of crossing over into Mexico where they would be safe from any pursuit by US law officers. But not by a vengeance-driven nemesis like Matt Devlin.

Matt spurred ahead. They were a few days ahead so there was no time to lose if he were to catch them on this side of the border. But how long would Patch wait for his men to turn up? That was the question.

Around mid-morning, he crested a rise to see a church rising out of the flat desert plain down below. This must be the Tumacácori Mission.

There were numerous such sanctuaries dotted across the south west offering spiritual and more secular sustenance to weary travellers. They were run by Catholic monks.

This one had been completed in the early 1800s and stood on the site of an earlier one dating back to 1692 which had been destroyed by fire. The aim of the early missionaries was to convert the Indians to Christianity as well as securing Spanish dominance over the new world. Mission stations provided a sound means of settling the land through farming and adherence to Spanish laws.

A quick look told the newcomer that the place had been attacked, and recently, judging by the smoke rising from one of the outbuildings. Luckily the main structure was still untouched.

Not so those who had clearly made a fruitless attempt to drive off the invaders of their remote enclave. The bodies of three monks lay strewn about outside the main gate.

It occurred to Matt that those Apaches had found easier prey on which to vent their hostility. He spurred off down the slope, pushing the appaloosa up to the gallop. Maybe somebody was still alive. Diving out of the saddle, he made a rapid inspection of the bodies. But there was no help possible here. All were dead. The coarse brown of their habits was stained with blood.

But more significant was the grim fact that all had been gunned down. Not a single arrow nor war lance in sight. Matt cursed aloud. This had to be the doing of the skunks he was after.

After gingerly passing through the outer cordon, the rider led his horse up towards the grand edifice that dominated the harsh surroundings. Such grandiose buildings erected to the glory of God were intended to overawe the resident population of converts to the Catholic faith. In this they succeeded. Although, the Indians often prayed to their new god alongside the pagan deities of old. Brightly coloured patterns had even been painted on its outer frontage by the local Indian converts.

Matt pushed open the heavy main door and entered the hallowed portal. The shadowy haze slowly faded as his eyes became accustomed to the gloom. The interior was far more ornately decorated than his own rather austere Church of the Good Shepherd. Those of the Catholic faith went more for ritualism and ceremony than his own more puritanical leaning. There was no condemnation in Matt's focussed assessment.

'We're all Christians,' he muttered under his breath while moving up the centre aisle. 'And headed for the same final round-up . . .'

Any further observation was cut short by the arresting sight of an elaborately stained glass window depicting the crucifixion that encompassed the entire back of the church. Sun streaming in through the glass image told the story in all its brutal glory. But far more graphic was the sight of a real figure tethered on the main cross to one side of the altar.

Initially unseen by eyes ranging over the Lord's final hours, Matt shivered at this awful sight. His legs felt like jelly and almost gave way. A pillar saved him from being grounded. This must be how he himself had been found back in Firewall. A rippling dread of déjà vu coursed through his body.

The shock was accordingly all the more heartrending as his heart speeded up to that of a runaway train, unable to absorb the implications. Did this guy Patch have some repellent curse against those of a religious bent? The answer to that conundrum would only come to light when he challenged the perpetrator face to face. Head bowed, he prayed hard for the strength to carry on.

Suddenly, a low groan issued from the mouth of what he had thought was a dead priest. Hope flickered in his squinting gaze. The man was still alive! Quickly, he leapt to his feet, hurrying over to cut the badly injured man down from his torment.

The ageing priest looked older than the church he had once administered. A gnarled grey face bearing more furrows than a badly ploughed field creased up in agony. He struggled to raise himself, but fell back, the effort too much for the frail body to manage. His injuries were far more serious than Matt's own had been.

Heavy eyelids forcibly prised themselves open. A spark of acuity wavered in the pain-filled gaze. It was as if he recognized a fellow man of the cloth. Matt's arm was gripped by a surprisingly strong hand.

'They stole . . . the Cross of San Xavier,' he croaked out. 'It . . . is solid gold. I tried . . . to resist. But my body . . . was too weak.' He fell back, exhausted by the effort. Momentarily he rallied. 'You must . . . find it, my son, and . . . bring it . . . back. My simple flock revere it. They will wither and die . . . without the cross as their . . . guide.'

'What is your name?' Matt asked.

'I am Father Antonio Serra.' Blood dribbled from between clenched teeth. The poor guy was near the end.

'Who did this?' Matt asked urgently.

The priest's watery regard faltered. But he summoned one final effort to rise. The weak voice was barely above a whisper, forcing Matt to lean in close. The priest's breathing was shallow and laboured. 'There were . . . three of them. The leader, they called him . . . Jack . . . '

Matt filled in the rest. 'Patch.' He gave a meaningful nod. 'I also am after this brigand. Do not worry, Father, I will catch them and return your icon to its true place.'

'It is good, my son . . . '

'Those men will answer to the Lord for their infamy. If not to Him, then to the devil himself.' But it was too late. The old priest could not hear. He had breathed his last on this earth.

Matt made the sign of the cross over the still body. It was not the mark of faith to which he subscribed, but this man deserved a holy blessing. He then mumbled a few words of condolence, finishing with ' . . . and may your soul now enter the Kingdom of Heaven.'

The brutalized corpse was carried outside to join the others of his calling. Of the so-called flock, there was no sign. They had clearly fled when the first shots were fired. It took the better part of two hours to dig graves and lay the four departed to rest. They were covered with stones for protection against wandering predators. Removing his hat, Matt commended their bodies to the ground with a suitable eulogy.

Inside, his whole being was suffused with an anger totally at variance to the forgiveness and reconciliation he had come to revere. The hideous death of his wife, and now that of Father Serra threatened to engulf him in its ravenous tentacles. And it was all down to the actions of one man and his gang.

His head lifted towards the brilliant azure of the sky. But no elation at the passing of the storm showed in the tight lines around his eyes. Hands raised, he threw out a chilling declaration. 'I'm coming for you, Jack Patch. You and that bunch of snakes. Wherever you are, there'll be no hiding place from the wrath of Matthew Devlin. And I won't rest until you're all in that place where fire and brimstone rule supreme.'

He sank to his knees, head bowed. And remained there lost in thought. It was the cawing of a buzzard perched on one of the wooden crosses he had fashioned that broke into the macabre visions clouding his addled brain.

Slowly, with great effort, he rose to

his feet. The faithful appaloosa had not moved. He walked over and stroked the noble head, receiving a salutary snicker of accord.

'If only life were as simple for me, pal, as it is for you,' he murmured into the twitching ear. Then he mounted up. There was not much light left. But Matt had no wish to spend the night in this lonely and besmirched enclave.

Leading his spare mount, he spurred off across the level sward towards the Tumacácori Mountains, anxious to be away from this brutal scene of devastation. His thoughts were filled with the unholy actions that Jack Patch had initiated.

7

Muscle Power

On the second day after departing from the Mission, Matt found himself entering broken country interspersed with rocky hummocks and clusters of towering organ pipe cacti. There was no trail and the ground was rough, forcing his pace down to a meandering plod amidst the rough undergrowth. Landmarks were considerably reduced which meant he had to navigate by keeping the sun as much as possible on his left side.

It was some time later with a silent prayer of thanks that he joined a well-used track heading in the right direction. The meandering trail gradually descended from the plateau through a tangle of palo verde trees. Much as they tried, the clutching branches failed in their quest to unseat the rider. Nonetheless, he was relieved to emerge from the enclosed woodland close to a river where a surprise awaited him.

There, on the far side, a lone wagon was struggling to climb the far bank of Tenmile Wash. The lumbering conestoga had managed to get across the fast flowing waters but was now trapped in thick mud where the emerging trail had been turned into a quagmire by the recent floods. The driver was ruthlessly applying his whip to urge the team of four onward. But the more he belaboured them, the deeper the narrow wheels were becoming encased in the clinging ooze.

A woman was vainly attempting to push the heavy wagon from behind. She pitched forward into the brown mess, unable to make more than an inch of headway. Scrambling to her feet, she once again applied herself to the onerous task. A mixed look of respect and cynicism indicated what he thought of the body-sapping endeavour. That said, he had to admit she was one game female.

It was a pity her efforts were proving to be futile, for the wagon was gradually slipping back towards the thrashing torrent. Matt cast an eye downstream. It did not look good. A hundred yards further on, white water rapids were a strong hint that catastrophe loomed should they fail. In their present situation, that was a distinct possibility. These folks badly needed help.

And he had two horses. Tether them up front and some much needed pulling power ought to save the day.

Once he had descended the rough slope, Matt instructed the driver to hold the team steady while he quickly roped up his two mounts alongside. So intent was the woman with her back-breaking toil, she failed to heed the arrival of assistance. She came round to see why her man had applied the brake.

'What's happening, Henry? Why have

we stopped?' Only then did she notice the tall stranger busily securing the much needed extra muscle power. Her mouth gaped wide. 'Who are you?' The query was edged with suspicion. 'And where'd you spring from out of the blue?'

'That's a heap of questions, ma'am, for a guy who's only trying to help you out.' Matt paused as an appreciative eye roamed across the mud-smeared apparition. She might not be dressed for a Thanksgiving Ball, but that clinging mud displayed her willowy contours to mesmeric effect. For a moment he was lost for words.

'Don't just stare, you big oaf,' the woman chastised the ogling watcher. 'Ain't you never seen a working female before?'

Matt couldn't help but chuckle uproariously. 'Guess not one in your condition, ma'am. And the name is Matt Devlin, at your service.' He gave her a chivalrous bow, flourishing his hat. 'Now if'n we're done jawing, perhaps we could get back to saving your wagon.'

'We sure appreciate your help, Mr Devlin,' the man said. 'My wife didn't mean no disrespect, did you, Laura?' He cast an admonishing look towards the scratchy dame. 'My name's Henry Douglas. We're hoping to reach Nogales where I intend setting up in the freighting business with this wagon. This is the right way, isn't it?'

Matt then shifted his attention to the speaker. This man sure wasn't dressed for the trail. He looked more like an office clerk. The obvious conclusion was that these two greenhorns were lost.

'Nice to meet you folks,' Matt replied, making no mention of his own intentions. 'As to your question. You're heading too far south. The trail you want branched off a day's ride back. But for the moment, I reckon we need to save this wagon or all your hopes are going to end up being washed down the river. You clean up, Mrs Douglas, then

104

climb on the wagon and take a breather.'

'I'll do no such thing,' she snapped. 'There'll be time enough to rest when the job's completed and not before.' Good looking to be sure, Matt thought, but Laura Douglas sure was one feisty dame. 'Like you say, mister, the main task now is to save this heap of junk, seeing as all our worldly goods are inside.'

The two men gave each other knowing looks that said this fireball was not the sort of woman to be pushed around. It was the sudden lurching of the wagon backwards that provided an urgent reminder that catastrophe was close at hand. Laura Douglas disappeared round the back to once again lend her insignificant weight to the arduous task.

'You ready, Douglas?' Matt called out. 'We need to do this together.'

The freighter nodded, gathering up the reins ready for the word. Matt raised a hand as he likewise made ready for the critical heave. 'On the count of three, we all pull together. One . . . two . . . three . . . '

A whip cracked, muscles of both men and beasts strained to the limits trying desperately to prevent the wagon from sliding back. Already the wheels were buried up to the axles in the cloying ooze.

'Come on, you lazy nags, get moving!' Douglas screamed, urging the team to herculean efforts essential to prevent disaster. Again the whip cracked over the heads of the straining beasts.

But to no avail. Even with two extra horses, the whole caboodle was losing ground. Matt realized there was only one way to prevent the looming debacle. 'Hold them on the brake,' he called out to the driver.

Without waiting for a reply, he leapt off his horse and dashed back to the rear. 'We need to lighten the load and chock up the back wheels,' hc told Laura Douglas, while scrambling up into the rear of the wagon. 'I'll throw down some boxes to stop the slide.' Grabbing hold of the nearest crate, he tossed it outside. 'You push them against the wheels.'

The woman hesitated. Her mouth dropped open. 'Those are my best clothes in there. You can't do that!'

'Do you want to end up stuck out here with nothing?' Matt caustically retorted. 'Cos that's what'll happen if'n we don't do something quick. There are dangerous rapids downstream from here that will smash this crate to matchwood. Now shift your butt, pronto. We can have a big clean up once your worldly goods have been saved. Here's another one.' A second box followed the first.

The vehemence in this man's urgent tone shocked the woman out of her haughty manner. She quickly shut her mouth and began handling the crates into position. Within minutes, the inevitable retreat had been halted. Matt jumped down.

'You done well, ma'am.' Matt's avid praise brought the first hint of a smile to Laura Douglas's mud-smeared countenance. 'Next thing is to toss some rocks in front to provide traction for the wheels.' The woman was breathing hard, her ample chest heaving. After all that had happened she was plumb tuckered out.

A softening of the hard exterior saw her saviour relenting. A kindly hand rested on her shoulder. 'Reckon you've done your share, Mrs Douglas. Take a breather. It's time us men took the strain.'

On this occasion, she merely nodded and slumped to the hard ground. The mud caking her face had dried to a hard carapace. But she still looked magnificent. Even more beautiful than before if such was possible. Matt quickly looked away. How could he be harbouring such licentious thoughts? His own wife barely in her grave and he was eyeing up another woman, and a married one to boot.

Shrugging off the devil whispering in his ear, Matt called out to the driver. 'I need you down here to help shift these rocks, Douglas.' The terse order received a sigh of disgruntlement but was nonetheless obeyed.

Once the layer of stone had been deposited at the front of all four wheels, Matt announced, 'OK folks, this is where we pray to the Lord that it's gonna be enough.' Both men scrambled back into their respective positions. Leathers firmly grasped, Douglas waited for the signal. When it came, together they urged the sweating horses to drag their heavy burden free of the grasping morass.

Yips and hollers echoed around the valley bottom as the team strove with all its might. And slowly but surely the wagon crept forward. Once it had gathered momentum, they were soon on dry ground. Cheers of joy rang out. It was a great feeling for all involved.

So overcome was Laura Douglas that she threw her arms around their good samaritan and kissed him firmly on the cheek. Once again, Matt felt those suppressed urges building inside his body. He desperately wanted to respond. The woman quickly sensed that she was going beyond the accepted norms of propriety and pulled away. She laughed to hide her discomfiture.

'Can't have you getting all mudded up like me. It'll take a few bars of soap to feel anywhere like normal again.'

Henry Douglas stepped down off the wagon and placed an arm around his wife's shoulders. 'Much obliged for all your help,' he said, making sure their saviour acknowledged the boundaries. 'Guess we owe you more than we can give. All we have is tied up in this venture. I've had to take odd jobs to keep us going. But we're both certain it was the right thing to do. Ain't that right, Laura?'

The woman nodded but her heart did not appear to match the aspirations of her husband. Matt could sense there were tensions here. The woman was a reluctant traveller. But that was none of his concern. His only thought should be the hunting down of Jack Patch and the rest of his gang.

But neither could he just abandon these greenhorns. They were clearly unprepared for the arduous journey being undertaken. Travelling alone across wild country populated by warring bands of Apache was the height of folly. A sensible and caring husband would have foreseen that and signed on with a wagon train.

An hour later, with their washed duds strewn across the roof of the covered wagon drying out, it was time to continue their journey.

'I'll ride along for a spell until you're back on the right trail,' Matt declared without asking. 'Make sure you don't get into any more trouble. This is Indian country and a lone wagon will be an easy target impossible to resist.'

'That's very thoughtful of Mr Devlin, isn't it, Henry?' Laura purred, nudging her noncommittal spouse.

'Guess so,' Douglas replied, somewhat grudgingly. 'But I ain't no tenderfoot, mister. I can look after my own. Just so's you know.'

'I'm sure you can. But as I said, this is dangerous country, even for those of us who know it well. You'd do well to remember that.' He didn't wait for a reply, instead spurring ahead to check the trail.

'There was no need to be so tetchy with him, Henry,' the woman admonished her husband. 'We'd never have gotten out of that mess without his help.'

'I know that, woman,' came back the surly reply. 'But I saw the way he looked at you. Just keep your distance from that critter. That's all I'm saying.'

'You're imagining it. You always were a jealous man, even before we married,' Laura continued to chide her husband. 'And losing what little money we'd saved in that poker game in Willcox didn't help.'

'Will you stop bleating on about that?' Douglas rasped. 'As I've already told you a dozen times, I've made full provision for that which will come to fruition when we reach Nogales.'

'So you keep saying. When am I going to hear about this big surprise of your'n? So far it's only words.'

Henry Douglas huffed some, muttering under his breath. 'Best you don't know the details, Laura. All I'll say is that it will be the answer to all our problems.'

The woman glared at her husband, wondering how she had come to be mixed up with such a man. 'That means it has to be something shady, underhanded.'

Henry Douglas remained tight-lipped about his so-called deal, immediately changing the subject. 'Reckon after all that pandemonium down at the river, we need a rest and some grub. And I could sure use a drink.' He drew the team to a halt.

'That's your answer to everything,

isn't it, Henry? Reaching for a bottle.'

But Laura Douglas had made her bed, and was not one for opting out of her responsibilities. A strict Baptist upbringing had drilled that into her at an early age. She stepped down off the wagon and began preparing the evening meal. No more was said about the incident at Tenmile Wash.

Over a surprisingly pleasant meal prepared by Laura Douglas, her husband regaled their saviour of his lack of success in obtaining suitable employment which was the reason they were headed for the border.

'Folks told me that trade with Mexico is highly profitable. They want our dollars, and are prepared to sell goods cheaply to obtain the currency. It should be a win-win situation for us down there.'

The tales of bad luck that were always the fault of someone else received regular nods of commiseration. Yet in truth, they fell on deaf ears. At least Arby Tench had been right on one thing. A guy made his own luck in this world. Anything went wrong, it fell on his shoulders to do something about it.

It was the woman who was once again impinging herself on his thoughts. Try as he might, he could not ignore her soft body momentarily laid against his. He shook off the guilty feeling, instead focussing on the coming days and where they would lead him. Once again he tried listening to Henry Douglas's grumbling lamentation.

These two were an odd pairing. A comely dame such as Laura Douglas tied in with this shifty dude. Some unions were a mystery known only to the participants. As a preacher, Matt had officiated at many such alliances. And he was still no nearer learning the secret of undying love. It took all sorts to make a world. All he knew was that his own marriage had truly been a match made in Heaven.

Next morning, the two travellers accompanied by their guardian, made an early start. They soon dropped down on to a level sward of salt pans known as Presidio Flats. It was a dry arid wilderness with no shade. Matt informed his associates that if they stuck to the edge of the Flats, they would reach the main trail for Nogales come sundown. Laura Douglas was forced to remain inside the wagon. The heat reflecting off the white pans was so intense.

Around noon, a distant cloud of fermenting white heralded the approach of riders. Matt drew his revolver, instructing Douglas to likewise arm himself. 'Never know who you might meet out here,' the sentinel warned. 'Always best to be prepared.'

In the event, it soon became apparent that an army patrol was approaching. In the lead was an officer flanked by a sergeant with twenty troopers following behind in pairs. The officer announced himself as Captain Jeremiah Thoroughgood, working out of Fort Defiance on the far side of the Dragoons.

'We're hunting down a band of

renegade Mescaleros that have been causing trouble hereabouts,' he informed the travellers. 'They burnt down a homestead over in Papago Canyon and murdered the farmer and his wife. You ain't come across them by any chance, have you? Their leader wears a black high crown and is called Shonto.'

It was Matt who answered. 'I've heard about him. I had a run in with some bucks a few days back. But all they seemed to want was my horse. Once I backed off they fell on it like a pack of wolves. These guys were only armed with bows and arrows and just looked like a hunting party to me.'

'Can't be the varmints I'm after,' the officer replied. 'Shonto is one mean son of a bitch. Pardon my language, ma'am. But he ain't known for taking prisoners, just scalps. Ain't that right, sergeant?'

'Sure is, sir,' piped up the burly three-striper. 'He and some others busted out of the reservation a month back and have been ravaging the country ever since. We need to catch those critters soon before they kill more settlers.'

'You folks shouldn't be out here all alone like this,' Thoroughgood added. 'You're setting yourselves up as sitting ducks for Shonto and his bunch to attack. Where are you headed?'

'My wife and I are aiming to reach Nogales. This man helped us out of a tough spot when our wagon got stuck crossing Tenmile Wash yesterday. But he has other business and will be leaving us soon.'

Thoroughgood brushed their intentions aside with a cynical look towards his sergeant. 'This is no place for a woman. My advice is to head east for the nearest town. And that's Benson. You can join up with one of the haulage companies if'n you're still intent on heading south for the border.'

'That's our objective and I don't see any need to change it,' Douglas said, shrugging off the proffered suggestion. 'We haven't seen any sign of Indians since we set off from Willcox last week.'

'Well, all I can say is you're darned fortunate. But my betting is that your luck will run out if'n you carry on ahead.' A languid arm waved towards the bleak terrain. 'As you can see, there ain't a shred of cover out there to offer protection if'n Shonto decides to attack, which he surely will sooner or later. Anyway, it's your decision. We have work to do. *Adios*, folks.'

Captain Thoroughgood saluted the two men and tipped his hat to the lady before spurring off to continue the search for the renegades.

'He's right,' Matt declared. 'As I told you before. I reckon it would be wise to take the alternative route east of the Dragoons once you hit the main trail. It's longer by about three days. But at least your husband won't have his hair lifted before he sees you being carried off as some buck's trophy.' Laura stifled a cry of alarm. 'I'm sorry to frighten you, ma'am. But it's best you know the truth. That officer wasn't exaggerating.

Apaches have a deep rooted hate of the white man because of our invasion of their lands.'

But Douglas was adamant. 'I won't be side-tracked,' he insisted with uncharacteristic firmness. 'We need to reach Nogales soon. Any more delay and the deal I'm hoping to secure might not be up for sale. So we're going on.' He immediately whipped up the horses and moved off.

Matt just sat his horse, watching the wagon draw ahead. His brow creased into a puzzled frown. Something wasn't right here. Why was this guy so all-fired stubborn? He felt sure it was more than just some chance opportunity in Nogales. And more to the point, why place his and his wife's life at risk for a few extra days' travel? It didn't make sense.

Then he shrugged. It was their business, as was his bounden duty to accompany them, at least until they were out of danger. Much as he would have preferred to push on at a faster pace, Matt felt he had been given no choice in the matter. Yet deep down, he secretly welcomed the chance of sticking close to this woman who had awakened a yearning he scarcely wanted to admit.

8

Mixed Blessings

Another day passed without incident. There had been no sign of the alleged renegades.

'That soldier boy was talking a load of hot air,' scoffed Douglas. 'We ain't seen hide nor hair of a durned redskin.'

'That don't mean there aren't any around,' countered the reluctant guardian somewhat irritably. 'Mescaleros are like shadows. You only find out they're there when it's too late. So keep your eyes peeled and that gun handy.'

He had barely finished speaking when a whooping that could only have come from the throats of a band of Indians could be heard on the far side of a ridge.

'There! Hear that?' exclaimed Matt. 'What did I tell you? And it sounds like they're attacking some poor sucker at this very moment.'

It was lucky for the three travellers that earlier in the day they had avoided the obvious route through a ravine Matt had deemed too narrow for the wagon. This parallel course on the far side of the ridge could be seen to merge further ahead.

'Stay here while I take a look,' Matt ordered the wagon driver. 'And no talking. Sound travels on the wind in these canyons.'

He spurred up to the crest of the ridge and peered over the rim. A lone rider emerged from the cutting into open terrain. He was being pursued by a group of ten Apache warriors. And half of them were armed with rifles. Not the latest repeaters, these were single shot Spencers and a couple of Sharps. But they were good enough to do serious damage to anyone caught in the firing line.

In the lead was a brave sporting a distinctive black trophy hat. This had to be Shonto. More important, the Indians were steadily closing the gap.

The unequal race was heading directly below the spot where Matt was concealed. Dismounting, he took careful aim with his rifle. But before the attackers got within range, a lucky shot brought the rider's horse down.

He tumbled out of the saddle but managed to scramble behind the dead horse. Unlike on the recent occasion when Matt had been in a similarly precarious situation, these bucks were in rampant mood. They were fully painted up which meant that only the scalp of the white man would satisfy their blood lust.

Matt suddenly noticed he was in a tricky position. The Indians had abandoned their ponies some one hundred yards back and were moving stealthily forward. To save the guy from certain death, he would have to circle around behind them. No easy task without being spotted.

Fortunately, there was plenty of

cover. Keeping low, he ducked between clumps of juniper bushes and rocky outcrops, all the time keeping a wary eye on the assailants. None chose to look his way. All of their attention was focussed on what they assumed was their only quarry.

One of the renegades who had managed to outflank the cowering victim posed an immediate threat to the trapped man's continued enjoyment of life. He stepped out into the open, brandishing a lethal skinning knife in his right hand. Matt quickly took aim with his rifle and pumped a couple of shots at the buck. The Indian was stopped in his tracks, just before he lunged at the target. He threw up his arms with a scream.

But the shots had alerted his buddies who now turned to face this unexpected assault. The surprise visitor kept his head down. Two more rapid fire shots from his current position, followed by two more a short distance beyond, convinced the assailants they were under attack from a force much larger than one single combatant.

'Aaaagh! What is this? We have been tricked. The white eye is not alone.' Shonto, their leader, backed off, panning his rusty old Springfield from side to side.

Matt helped to further the ruse by calling out in the brusque guise of Captain Thoroughgood. 'Take three men, sergeant, and surround these bucks. Don't let them get away.' More grunted orders followed in a different voice, allegedly that of the non-com. 'Jackson and Smith, come with me. You other troopers give us covering fire. And make every shot count.'

Another Indian went down in a tangle of flailing limbs. This encouraged the victim of the strike to join in the counter attack even though he had been wounded by an arrow sticking out of his shoulder. With his good hand, he could only manage a single shot which was well off target. Nonetheless, the subterfuge had thrown the Indians into total disarray.

Convinced that the army had arrived, that was enough for Shonto. The Apache chief scuttled over to where his pony was tethered and leapt on to its back. 'Flee, my brothers, before it is too late. It is those accursed blue coats. There are too many of them.' The remaining Apaches needed no further encouragement. They were pursued by a hail of bullets as they fled the scene of conflict.

The object of the assault stood up and tried to cheer. But he fell to the ground. The wound was not life threatening but it was leaking blood fast. Matt hurried across and helped the guy back on to his feet.

'Much obliged for that, mister,' the injured man groaned, breathing heavily. 'Reckon I'd have been a goner for sure if'n you hadn't moseyed along. Those critters were after my hair and I'm mighty attached to it.' He cast a rheumy eye at his rescuer. 'You a scout for the army?'

'No such luck, fella,' was the chuckled response. 'That was only me doing a bit of play-acting. And it worked a treat. Never figured I had the knack.'

'Well, it sure frightened them away and no mistake.' The man smiled. 'Reckon you've discovered a new occupation on the stage.'

Before Matt could reply, the man reeled unsteadily as the pain of his wound took charge. He clung to his benefactor for support. In so doing, he accidently ripped Matt's shirt, revealing the wooden cross. His eyes widened. He'd seen that elaborately carved depiction somewhere else, and recently. For a moment his addled brain couldn't bring it to mind.

Then the awful shock of realization suddenly dawned. His saviour was none other than that preacher whose wife Klute had violated. Clad in range gear and without that moustache, Blackie Hayes would never have eyeballed the guy. Yet here he was. Even for a wounded jasper it took no brainpower to deduce why the fella was passing through this remote neck of the woods. He was out for revenge on the gang who had done him and his kin a bad hurt. And that most certainly would include Blackie Hayes.

He silently cursed his suggestion to branch off the main trail after the thunder storm. He should have stuck with the others, or at least persuaded his pal Greylag to join him. But that was then, this was now. No sense crying over spilt milk. Hayes knew there was only one way out of this mess.

Unfortunately for Matt, he had not recognized this man as one of those he was hunting. Blackie Hayes had remained in the shadows throughout the altercation in the church that had led to the preacher being pistol whipped into unconsciousness. The steely-eyed look of menace went unheeded as Matt turned his back to retrieve his horse. Hayes had not in any way condoned the young hothead's rash act of debauchery. But neither had he voiced any dissent. He had been wet and hungry at the time and that was all that mattered.

But he knew there could only ever be one outcome to this guy turning up out of the blue. So it was him or the preacher. And Blackie Hayes intended making his way to Nogales and enjoying the fruits of the gang's latest venture.

'You rest easy while I get my horse,' Matt said innocently, with not the slightest inkling as to the sinister intentions quickly being formulated inside the devious rat's mind. 'Leave that arrow be until I can remove it properly.'

Hayes remained silent, his thin lips parting in a looming grimace. Slowly he drew his pistol and quietly thumbed back the hammer. The gun lifted, pointing directly at the preacher's back. The trigger finger tightened. An explosion once again ripped apart the heavy silence that had descended over the canyon.

But it was not Matt Devlin who keeled over. The shock-induced gaze of Blackie Hayes told of his disbelief at the outcome of the bushwhacking. A second shot finished him off. Matt swung around and dropped to one knee, his own gun palmed and ready. But there was no need to use it. Hayes tumbled over and lay sprawled in an untidy heap across a clump of mesquite.

The intended victim of the sneaky attack was no less stunned by the guy's decision to kill his saviour. What had prompted the inexplicable behaviour? Maybe the arrow wound had curdled his brain. That was irrelevant now. Of far more importance as far as Matt was concerned lay with the identity of his lifesaver.

A movement over to his left caught Matt's attention. His gun shifted as another man stepped out from behind some boulders. He was a tough looking raw-boned jigger, dark of face and sporting a Mexican style moustache.

He strolled across the open sandy tract, leading a handsome bay mare with one hand, a smoking long gun in the other ready to deliver the final denouement should it be necessary. He idly poked at the sprawled heap. But Blackie Hayes would not be joining his buddies in Nogales.

The newcomer's narrow gaze then settled on the jasper he had just saved from a certain appointment with the Scythe Man. A puzzled frown brought lowering bushy eyebrows together as a less than welcome recollection of his own impinged on to the hard features.

'Just my luck to go and rescue Iron Matt Devlin.' The rescuer shook his head in mock admonishment of his error of judgement. 'If'n I'd known it was you in line for a dose of lead, perhaps I'd have let this critter do his worst.'

Matt stepped forward, equally non-plussed by the sudden reprieve. A leery grin split the craggy façade. 'Well, I'll be darned,' he declared. 'If'n it ain't that ugly cuss, Geery Vandyke! Must be all of three years since we last had dealings.'

Also known as the Dutchman, Vandyke was much more certain of the date on which this guy had tricked him out of a sizeable bounty. 'Two years, nine months and . . . ' A finger tapped his chin as if to emphasize how needled he felt. 'Yep, that's right, six days to be precise. A guy never forgets when a fellow man hunter does the dirty on him.'

The two men stood opposite one another, some ten feet apart. Muscles were tight, ready should the need arise for a gun down.

'I'd say that was a real mean trick to pull, creeping into a guy's camp and stealing his mark. Reb Dillard was worth a cool three thousand bucks. So I reckon you owe me, Devlin.' A sneer crossed the bounty man's gnarled features. 'And that ain't the first time as I recall. You beat me to Purgatory by two days. That two grand for Pecos Bob

Shadley was gonna be a deposit on a spread I was after.'

Matt ignored the accusation. 'In our game, a fella takes his chances where he finds them. You should never have left Dillard tied to that tree while you had your wicked way with that Apache squaw. I hope she was worth it.'

Now it was Vandyke's turn to be contrite. 'Ugh!' he grunted. 'Don't make me laugh. This is what I ended up with for my trouble.' He pointed to a pair of white lines on his left cheek. 'She was one helluva firecracker. Slippery as a wet fish before I finally tamed her. And when I came back, Dillard had vanished.' He slapped his thigh in exasperation at the sore memory. 'I tell you, mister, at that moment I was mad as a scalded cat. And I ain't forgot. It took me six months to find out who the thief was.' A frosty atmosphere hung in the air. 'Been hoping to bump into you ever since. Now ain't this my lucky day?'

But Matt had no inclination to cause

trouble. This man had saved his life and he had no quarrel with the Dutchman, even though Vandyke held a grudge he had been nursing for some while. He held up his hands. 'I don't want trouble, Dutch. Those days are past. I've moved on. I figure you have as well. Why don't we call it quits?'

Yet he couldn't resist a gentle dig. After all, they weren't best buddies. Never had been. Rivals in the same trade more like.

'It ain't exactly your style, Dutch, to step in and settle another man's problem,' he added casually while carefully lowering his gun hand to indicate his appreciation. 'Seeing as how you don't exactly hold me in high regard. So how come you decided to change the habit of a lifetime?'

'Maybe you're right. Could be I have mellowed over the years,' Vandyke declared, sitting down on a rock and rolling a couple of quirlies, one of which he handed to Matt. They lit up, the tension between them appeared to have thawed. Momentarily at least. Then he nodded towards the cross hanging round his old sparring partner's neck. 'I heard tell you'd quit the bounty caper and taken up preaching. Must have been that greaser kid who got in the way. So what you doing out here, toting a gun and a long way from home? Mighty strange, I'd say, for a man of the cloth.'

'I got my reasons. And they ain't up for discussion.' Matt certainly had no intentions of explaining himself to Dutch Vandyke. 'Let's just say my business will be concluded at the end of this trail.'

'And where might that be?'

'Now that would be telling. But I sure as Hell ain't on a mission to save any souls.'

'Seems like we could be heading in the same direction,' Vandyke announced in a conspiratorial tone. 'Although my aim and your'n are likely to be as different as chalk and cheese.'

'What you getting at, Dutch?'

'Maybe you ain't heard. You being a bit rusty and all when it comes to keeping a check on the lawless activities of our more wayward associates. But this jasper was a member of the Patch Gang. His name is Blackie Hayes.'

At that, Matt sat up, his whole body tensing. He had failed to recognize Hayes but the outlaw had clearly remembered him. It must have been when he saw the cross.

'I see that you've heard about them,' his associate continued. 'But did you know they robbed a bank in Willcox of thirty big ones? I started out after the bounties on offer. But they're chicken feed compared to what's in that strong box. So I'm going for the big haul.' Vandyke leaned forward and puffed hard on the quirley. 'And I ain't taking on no partners.'

The threat was there. Unspoken yet clear as a new moon.

'So there's one down with five to go. And I know for a fact there's bounties on three of them fellas. Jack Patch is the highest followed by that young hothead Klute. There's one other but I ain't sure who that would be. You're welcome to take 'em in, strapped over a saddle if you so choose.'

'That's mighty obliging of you, Dutch.' Matt's reply was loaded with irony. 'Only one thing wrong with your figuring,' he espoused casually without elucidating.

'You've gotten me all of quiver with curiosity, old buddy. Spill.'

'There's only three of them left, not five like you thought.' That declaration certainly had the guy's attention. 'I caught up with two during that storm a few days back. Found them sheltering in a cave. Stroke of luck them being there. But we didn't leave together next day if'n you get my drift.'

Vandyke scratched his shock of sandy hair. 'You sure are full of surprises. So how about describing these dudes so's I know who to scratch off'n my list.'

'One was a lean bald fella, the other more on the short stocky side called

Arby. That mean anything to you?'

Vandyke nodded. 'Arby Tench and Bonehead. Those two critters won't be missed by the human race. And it means my task is gonna be all the easier. So if'n it's all right with you, reckon I'll string along seeing as you seem to know where these dudes are headed.' The Dutchman grinned, a wicked twist of the lips that boded no good for their future association. 'Don't matter none if'n you do object, I'm still trailing along. And I don't figure a man of the cloth will stop me, seeing as I just saved his hide.'

An apathetic shrug of the shoulders indicated Matt's reluctant acceptance of the situation, for now at least. He couldn't exactly order the guy to leave. 'So how's about satisfying my curiosity? Why help a stranger out who at the time you didn't know from Adam?'

Once he had fired up another smoke, Vandyke answered the question. 'I never did cotton to back-shooters. Scum of the earth if'n you ask me. A guy who can't face his opponent man to man don't deserve any mercy. I'm sure you would agree . . . Reverend.' The poignant implication was unequivocal. 'That dude is best left for the coyotes. And far as I know, he ain't carrying no bounty on his head. So there's three guys over yonder mountains whose corpses will substantially add to your parish funds when this fracas is done and dusted.'

The preacher matched the other guy's sardonic aside with studied indifference. He was well aware that any trust he placed in Geery Vandyke would be like inviting a sidewinder to supper. Still, for the time being, he would go along with the charade for as long as it lasted while keeping his eyes and ears well tuned in to any skulduggery. And that was proven with his next remark.

Vandyke toed the sand with his boot. Then slowly lifted the rifle. 'Looks like we'll get along fine, Reverend. Just so long as you don't have any ideas concerning that strong box.'

The two old associates stood facing each other across the sandy wasteland. Overhead a lone buzzard circled, its hungry cawing a sinister addendum to the build of tension.

'If'n you're figuring to haul off with that smoke-pole, Dutch, better consider whether you levered a fresh round into the breech,' Matt intoned in a flat monotone devoid of any anger. 'My guess is you didn't. Shall we find out?'

Vandyke chewed on his lower lip. The sour grimace melded to a sly smirk. 'Reckon you could be right there,' he murmured while slowly lowering the rifle. The hostile moment of discord had passed. He then began thumbing fresh rounds into the magazine. A knowing eye scrutinized the skyline. 'It's getting a mite late in the day for resuming our journey. What say we camp here for the night, old buddy?'

'What I say is that we ain't buddies,' Matt firmly declared. 'You saved my hide, and I'm beholden. But that's as far as it goes. We're both after the same thing, but for wildly different reasons. Sooner or later, that's gonna show itself. But for now, two guns are better than one around here.'

The distinct possibility that Shonto might well return hung in the air. An extra gun to deter any reprisals was welcome. He had little confidence in the gunfighting prowess of Henry Douglas. If anything, the guy was a hindrance he could well do without.

The guilt-laden notion once again raised its ugly head as to how a woman like Laura Douglas could have allied herself to such a guy. He threw it off. This was no time for harbouring such thoughts.

'Have it your own way.' The Dutchman shrugged. 'Best that a fella knows which side of the fence he's sitting on.'

Moments later, he received his second surprise of the day.

9

Devil's Grip, the Iron Fist

Trundling into view from around a nearby promontory was a wagon pulled by four horses. Two people were sitting up front.

'Where in thunderation did that spring from?' Geery Vandyke tossed a suspicious look towards his associate. 'You know anything about this, Devlin?'

'They're the reason I don't mind you tagging along for a spell,' Matt replied. 'I ran into them back at Tenmile Wash. Their wagon had gotten stuck in the mud. They ain't exactly trail broke. And with Shonto on the warpath, I figured to stick with them until we hit the main trail before leaving.'

The wagon had drawn closer, affording Vandyke an ample view of the occupants. He ignored the driver, a greenhorn if ever there was one in that store-bought suit. But the dame was something else entirely. He whistled in admiration. She was the purtiest thing he'd clapped eyes on in a coon's age.

Matt tried to hide a critical scowl. He couldn't help but pick up on the lustful aura leaching from every pore of the Dutchman's lean frame. Somehow he managed to curb his irritation, noting something else instead. Could he possibly be feeling jealous? Here was a rival for Laura Douglas's attention. The unsettling thought was transitory, but had been planted and would grow in the hours ahead.

As the wagon drew to a halt, Vandyke posed the same query again. 'What are you folks doing out in this wild country all alone?' Darkly accusatory eyes pinned the driver to his seat. 'I'd call that mighty reckless for a man accompanied by such a fine looking wife.'

Henry Douglas was not about to explain himself to yet another stranger on the trail. He purposely ignored the query. 'We heard all that shooting after Mr Devlin went off to investigate,' he explained, ignorant of the disturbing undercurrent his beautiful wife was exerting. 'And then there was silence. We didn't know what had happened. All we could do was hang on for a spell.'

His wife continued with the clarification. To Vandyke's ears her velvet tone was smooth and silky like melted chocolate.

'When you didn't return . . . ' Her contribution was aimed at Devlin. The other guy gave her the creeps. His dissolute gaze followed her every movement. ' . . . we decided it would be best to find out for ourselves how things stood.'

Devlin went on to outline the course of events that had led to his meeting with Geery Vandyke. The man saving his life, although somewhat suspect, was given due credence. 'We figure after all the action today, it might be better to make camp here then have an early start in the morning,' Devlin added.

'I'm sure Mrs Douglas here is right handy with a skillet and saucepan. Ain't that so, ma'am?' Vandyke's intimation, accompanied by that shifty grin, was received with imperious indifference. 'My stomach's rumbling like thunder. I ain't eaten a thing for two days. Been living off rabbit and the last of my beans. Last good meal I had was in Willcox on the far side of the mountains.'

Mention of the town brought a hint of nervousness to Henry Douglas. Matt picked up on the greenhorn's discomfort again, wondering as to its origins.

'If you are in a hurry to get somewhere, Mr Vandyke, don't let us stop you.'

Laura's mordant suggestion went over the head of the thick-skinned hardcase. 'Nothing that won't keep, ma'am. Ain't that so . . . old pal?'

Matt ignored the ill-concealed jibe as he helped with setting up the camp.

Later that evening after a particularly

delicious supper, the four disparate travellers were seated round the campfire. Vandyke was relaxing with a cigar.

'Gee, ma'am, that sure was a feast fit for a king.' He smacked his lips in appreciation then tossed in the hint that Henry Douglas had taken on too much dragging his wife out here into the wilderness. 'Takes the right sort of guy to venture out into wild country like this. Especially when there's bloodthirsty Indians around. You that sort, Douglas?'

His wife butted in on her husband's behalf. 'We are both more than capable of handling the rigours involved in this journey,' she averred with a firm assurance. 'I love my husband and have every confidence in his ability to get us safely to our destination.'

The callous tough was not the only one present who also harboured such a notion as to the driver's capabilities. But Matt Devlin kept his own counsel.

'Love. Now ain't that a strange word,' Vandyke sardonically mused.

'Don't reckon guys like Matt here and me are gentle enough to have it in us. Shall I tell you how Iron Matt here earned his nickname?'

Raised eyebrows greeted this unexpected piece of news which he took as an affirmative. 'That's right. Guys in our line of work call him Iron Matt.' Without waiting for the man in question to comment, Vandyke launched into the story. 'He was courting this gal up in Flagstaff. It was some years back now. Another guy decided he wanted to muscle in and started hassling her. Matt wasn't too pleased about that. He asked the guy politely to disappear, but to no effect. That was enough for Matt. It only took the one punch. The guy was laid out cold. And you know what?'

He never got to finish the story. Matt was all steamed up. Suddenly, he jumped to his feet and grabbed a hold of the narrator, hauling him to his feet.

'You've said enough, mister. More than enough. Now I reckon it's time you left. You've outstayed your welcome.'

Vandyke's laugh emerged more as a cynical grunt. 'The truth hurts, I guess. Don't you folks want to hear how the story ended?' Vandyke called out, allowing himself to be manhandled over to his mount.

'No, they don't,' Matt snapped. 'Now mount up and skedaddle before I . . . '

But Vandyke was not finished. He pulled free of the firm grip.

'Before you what, Iron man? Give me the same treatment? Is that it?' A scowl of disdain intimated what he thought of that suggestion. 'These people deserve to hear the grim truth about the guy who's helping them. You see, folks, nice, gentle Matt here had killed that guy stone dead with his fist. A single punch shut the guy's lights out for good. Don't reckon he ever got over that. Did you, old buddy? Made him turn to the Good Book for consolation. But that ain't the main reason he found God. Why don't you tell them about that kid you shot down in Purgatory?'

The disparaging Dutchman was enjoying seeing his old adversary squirm. The challenge found Matt taking a lunge at his old rival. The legendary fists bunched, ready to deliver their mayhem. Vandyke managed to dodge a solid right and quickly mounted up. Now thoroughly incensed, Matt tried to drag the guy off his horse. But a drawn revolver stayed his hand.

'If'n it weren't for the presence of this good lady, I'd drill you in the guts like I should have done back there.' He leaned forward over the neck of his horse, a menacing jab of the pistol keeping his rival at bay. 'But make no mistake, preacher man, this ain't the last you've seen of Geery Vandyke. I'll be back. And guess who'll be in my sights. Next time I won't hold back.'

With that parting shot, he spurred off into the gathering gloom. A macabre burst of laughter sent shivers down Laura Douglas's spine. The sudden upsurge of animosity had left both she

150

and her husband completely non-plussed.

Matt walked away, unable to face this woman whose esteem he so much valued. Guilt in all its dark forms washed over him. He cursed the Dutchman for resurrecting old wounds that he had thought were well and truly buried in the past. How wrong could you be? A cigar helped to calm his jangled nerves. Dutch Vandyke had hit a sore spot, and it hurt bad.

Sometime later, he didn't know how long, a light touch on his arm brought Matt out of his gloomy meditation. He knew instinctively who it was. The musky scent of this alluring woman was a challenge to all those moral values he held dear. God was testing him. Would he be able to resist?

The soft tone eased the tension building inside him. 'She must have been a special woman, your wife. You must miss her greatly.'

Over supper the previous night, Matt had reluctantly told Laura why he was heading for Nogales. The truth had been slowly but delicately dragged out of him, although the gruesome details of the horrendous event had been substantially condensed in the telling. Talking through the incident had helped him to reconcile his ultimate objective of running the culprits to ground, allowing his conscience to settle.

The tall stranger peered out into the gloom of night. 'Vandyke was wrong when he said guys like us could never feel love. But Sarah is dead.' With difficulty he managed to gulp down the bitterness of the memory. 'After gunning down that kid in Purgatory, all I wanted was for the ground to swallow me up. Then I met her. It was at a Saturday dance in Tucson. You could say it was love at first sight. Now all that has been destroyed.'

His eyes misted over. Laura Douglas gripped his arm, empathizing with the loss. Once he had recovered his composure she purposefully stepped away.

'But nothing can bring her back. And life has to go on.' He then looked deep into this enchanting woman's eyes.

An intense yearning to take her in his arms threatened to overwhelm them both. It was Laura who drew a line across the awkward moment. 'You will meet somebody else. Somebody who can help rebuild your life. Mine is with Henry. I know he appears weak at times and ill-suited for a life on the frontier. But he loves me, and I love him.' Once again she squeezed Matt's arm, then turned and walked away.

The curtain had been drawn. Matt once again stared out into the opaque void of gathering darkness. They had reverted to mere travellers thrown together by circumstance. Nothing more, nor less. Matt was relieved that the heartfelt dilemma had been removed. His conscience was clear, and all at the behest of Laura Douglas. He owed her for that.

His hand strayed to the cross beneath his shirt. It now had the hard touch akin to a cross of iron. *Vengeance is mine, saith Matt Devlin!*

When it was time to settle down for the night, Matt took the first watch. There was no knowing if those renegade Apaches would attempt a night attack. Some Indians felt it was bad medicine, others shunned the notion. Who could tell what was in Shonto's mind? And then there was Geery Vandyke. He might decide to avenge his humiliation at being shown up in front of the woman sooner than expected.

Dawn broke with no sign of any predators, unless of course you counted the odd coyote sniffing around. An early start found them on the trail once again. Throughout the morning, Henry Douglas had spoken barely a word. He kept casting shifty looks towards their guardian. Could he suspect what had been in Matt's thoughts since he first laid eyes on Laura? There was only one way to find out. They arrived at the break of trail around noon.

Matt called a halt. 'This is where we part company, folks. I'm cutting across country to save time. I don't trust Vandyke one inch. He could easily throw in with Patch and his boys. And I don't want you folks getting caught in the crossfire.'

Douglas merely grunted. His manner was beginning to grate on Matt's nerves. 'If'n there's something bothering you, mister, let's have it out in the open. You've been like a bear with a sore head all day.'

Laura had likewise picked up on her husband's withdrawn manner. She waited for her man to voice what she expected was a jealous harangue against the concern she had shown for their fellow traveller. Both of them held the same notion as to what was on Henry Douglas's mind.

'It's nothing,' he replied. 'I'm just worried those Indians might turn up again.'

'You're on the main trail now.' Matt breathed a sigh of relief, assuaging his concern. 'They usually stick to the lesser known routes to avoid army patrols. But keep your guns handy just the same.'

'You will be careful, won't you, Matt?' Laura's petition was heartfelt and genuine. This man had helped them. And she knew he was heading into a potential clash with some violent adversaries.

He smiled. 'I have the Lord on my side, ma'am. He won't let me down.' With a tip of his hat, the tall rider spurred off into the unknown.

Knowing what he did, Henry Douglas was glad to see him leave. Sitting on a small fortune was grating on the nerves. He would be glad to turn it over to Jack Patch and receive his share of the proceeds. Laura on the other hand was torn between her love for the man next to whom she was sitting and the enigmatic stranger who had unwittingly stumbled into her life. Would she ever lay eyes on him again? It was a quandary she was loath to pursue.

10

Bad News for Vandyke

Geery Vandyke approached the border town of Nogales with his senses on full alert. He knew that Jack Patch and his two remaining associates would be somewhere close by. It was highly unlikely that they would recognize him. On the other hand, sporting his trademark eye mask, the gang boss would be easy to spot.

The place was heavily influenced by its proximity to Mexico. Particularly overpowering was the pungent scent of animal dung emanating from the huge bull ring on the outskirts of the town. Contests between matador and bull were a much favoured pastime pursued by those of Spanish descent.

Moving past the holding pens and along the main street, adobe buildings with Spanish names predominated. Stetson-wearing American adventurers intermingled with hombres of a swarthy appearance hidden beneath wide sombreros and clad in apparel redolent of those originating from south of the border. Hanks of red chilli peppers hung everywhere, drying in the sun.

On the surface, the town gave out a colourful and exotic mix. But the newcomer was well aware that violence between the opposing factions could flare up at the twitch of an eyebrow. Vandyke would need to walk a fine line, be on his guard at all times. His hand rested on his gun while moving slowly along the busy main street.

Nogales was a bustling place as befitted a border town. There was much coming and going. Wagons piled high with trade goods filled the narrow thoroughfare. Henry Douglas, assisted by his lovely wife, would no doubt be able to establish a successful freighting enterprise here. But then there was that irritating boil of a gunfighting preacher that needed lancing. While Matt Devlin still drew breath, the Dutchman could not rest easy.

Vandyke dismounted, tied off and went into the nearest saloon. The Picador was a rough and ready dump with few embellishments. In keeping with the town's favourite pastime, a large bloodthirsty mural of a contest between man and beast hung on the back wall. Gambling tables filled one side of the room. On the other was a bar, no more than half a dozen planks of sawn timber nailed to three upright beer barrels.

A sultry, raven-haired warbler sashayed about on a small stage accompanied by three energetic guitar players. Numerous bawdy comments from the drink-soused audience made lewd suggestions that the girl strove to ignore.

Vandyke was more concerned to find out whether his quarry was still in Nogales. He sauntered over to the bar. There was no draught beer on tap so he ordered a bottle of tequila. A couple of slugs were needed to help him decide how best to tackle the thorny issue of lifting the dough and removing all opposing factions with him, the last man standing. After sinking the third glass, he called to the bartender.

'Over here, *amigo*.' The fat Mexican wandered across. 'Have you seen a gringo hanging around town with a black patch over one eye?' he asked, slipping a silver dollar across the bar. 'There are two other jaspers with him.'

The greaser twitched his moustache in thought. 'Maybe I have, *señor*. But there again, maybe not.' The Dutchman sighed but nonetheless slid another dollar across the bar. The 'keep snatched it up, peered around slyly, then leaned across, whispering in a highly confidential manner. 'I think the *hombres* you are seeking, *señor*, have just walked through the door.'

Vandyke's avid gaze followed that of the barman. 'Much obliged, *amigo*.' Another coin dutifully followed the other two. Then he levered his lanky frame off the counter and made his way over to where the three men were standing.

Always alert to anything of a suspicious nature, Jack Patch immediately spotted the approaching American, including the low-slung gun rig. He nudged Greylag, indicating for his sidekick to stand to one side. Klute shifted over to the left, a protective measure against any trickery should the need arise. All three men laid hands on the butts of their own hardware.

Vandyke noticed the cagey manoeuvre and raised his hands to show he meant them no harm. He handed over the bottle of tequila, nodding towards a free table. 'I ain't looking for trouble, boys,' he avowed, sitting down opposite the gang boss. 'But I do have some important news you might want to hear.'

Still Patch remained silent, watching the newcomer like a hawk. It was Klute who broke the impasse. 'You got something to say, mister, best get it off'n your chest, pronto. We don't cotton to guys muscling in on our space uninvited.'

That was the moment Patch chose to intervene. 'Klute's right. I don't know who you are, fella. Or where you've sprung from. So what could you possibly know that would interest us?'

'The name's Geery Vandyke.'

Patch shrugged indifferently. The name clearly meant nothing to him or Klute which suited the Dutchman fine. Keeping out of the limelight suited Vandyke's purpose. In fact, it was a bonus. He suppressed a smile.

Only Greylag appeared to show any interest. 'You ain't related to that Dutch painter by any chance, are you, mister?' The older brigand prided himself on being more of a serious bookworm than the others.

The newcomer scoffed. 'Only artistry I do is on a Saturday night when I like to paint the town red.' He chuckled at his own witticism.

None of the listeners joined in. Patch arrowed a look of censure at the grey outlaw. 'Just get to the point, Vandyke,' he spat. 'What's your angle?'

The smile remained pasted on the intruder's face. What he had to say would soon wipe the sneering look of contempt from this cocky rooster's face, shake him to the core. Having his gang chopped in half would be a serious setback to Jack Patch. Poor odds to be sure when facing off a guy like Matt Devlin.

In a much quieter voice Vandyke declared, 'That stunt you pulled in Willcox has gotten the authorities in a right sweat.'

Patch and Greylag both stiffened. 'What's that to you?' the boss snapped.

But the notoriety of their heist brought a proud smirk to Klute's boyish face. 'Hey, Jack, we're famous,' he preened. 'Ain't that some'n to crow about?'

'Not when it brings a real mean sonofabitch down on your heads, it don't,' said the newcomer. 'Remember that preacher you pinned up on a cross in Firewall? Well, he — '

Mention of that ill-fated incident saw Patch sitting forward. 'What in thunder do you know about that?' he snarled, cutting the other man off short.

Vandyke ignored the blunt demand for an explanation. 'That wasn't exactly a clever move, Jack.'

'Cut the smart talk, buster, and get to the point,' said Greylag, waving his shooter under the Dutchman's nose. All three outlaws were now becoming edgy, shifting nervously in their seats. This unknown interloper knew a sight too much about their affairs.

'Ever heard of a bounty man called Iron Matt Devlin?' Startled expressions indicated that the name had struck home. 'Well, he finished with the man hunting game two years back to take up preaching. A guilty conscience over some greaser kid he plugged. But you killing his wife has turned the guy's head, made him mad as a wounded puma. Forced him to take up the six-shooter again in place of the Bible. And he's after your blood. Every last one of you.'

The speaker paused, seeing that his mind-bending news had met with a vengeance. Klute in particular looked like he'd seen a ghost.

'And not only that. He's already started. A few days back, he removed two of your guys who were sheltering in a cave back in the Dragoon Mountains.'

'That must be Tench and Bonehead,' gasped the ashen-faced Klute.

'This guy means business, Jack,' muttered a nervy Greylag.

'I ain't finished yet.' Vandyke was enjoying himself seeing these jaspers squirm.

'Go on then!' Patch snapped irritably. This was going from bad to worse. 'What else do you know?'

'The Mescaleros got Blackie Hayes.' He felt it prudent to his continued good health not to mention his own part in the outlaw's demise. 'I witnessed it with my own eyes. Lifted his hair, they did. It's now gracing the war lance of a renegade called Shonto.'

These disclosures had thoroughly rattled the three outlaws. But Patch now revealed his gritty tenacity when the chips were down. 'You seem to know an awful lot for a guy just passing through, fella. Give me one good reason why I shouldn't plug you here and now. I don't cotton to guys who know all my business.'

The Dutchman had been expecting such a threatening reaction. But he was ready with an answer. 'That wouldn't be very wise, Jack. All that dough you stole back in Willcox ain't worth a plugged nickel if'n Devlin comes a-calling as he surely will. Now with you being short-handed, and me knowing where to find this jasper, I reckon it's in your best interests to take me on as a partner. An equal share of thirty grand cut four ways sounds fair to me. So what do you say?'

'I say we chop this guy up into little

pieces and feed him to the hogs,' snarled Klute, jumping to his feet.

A firm hand pulled the jittery kid back down into his seat. 'Keep your voice down, knucklehead. Do you want the whole town knowing why we're here? It's you that needs taking out, kid. You and that damned itchy pecker. But worse still, you then had to go and throttle the dame.'

'She started screaming, Jack,' whined the kid. 'I had to shut her up somehow.'

'If'n I didn't need your gun hand I'd darned well shut your big mouth up for good.' A look of withering contempt held Klute in his seat. 'But there's no sense in crying over spilt milk now. With three guys down, this needs thinking on.'

'Four including Smollett,' added a morose Greylag.

Jack Patch scowled. He didn't need reminding. His astute brain was tossing over the implications of what he had just learned. Having a guy like Iron Matt Devlin on his tail was not to be taken lightly. The skunk had to be removed from the picture.

He stood up and wandered across to the bar for another bottle.

It was clear from the sudden change in their fortunes that drastic action needed to be taken if they were to come out of this fracas smelling of roses. Back in his seat, he addressed Vandyke. 'How come you know so much about this bounty hunter?'

'I've been trailing him for some time, just waiting for the right moment to take him down. He done the dirty on me a while back. Thought I had him as well. But then he teamed up with a loan settler and his wife, helped pull their wagon out of Tenmile Wash.' It was a fabricated story but caught the gang leader's attention which was the main thing. 'We met up when I saved Devlin's hide after the Apaches jumped him. Big mistake on my part. I didn't recognize the critter until it was too late. But it sure made him beholden.' A wistful glint, a sigh of licentious hunger imbued the Dutchman's craggy visage.

'What's so funny?' snapped Patch, who was becoming edgier by the minute. 'This ain't no laughing matter.'

'Just thinking what a purty peach that Laura Douglas is,' he murmured. 'And Devlin had the hots for her as well. I could tell. We had a set to when I stuck a burr up his butt to lower his estimation in the dame's eyes. I would have drilled him there and then if'n it hadn't been for the woman. But his day will come. And he knows it.'

Vandyke scowled as he recalled the incident before continuing his story. 'Devlin is only escorting the Douglases as far as the main trail, then he's cutting across country to get here. And you guys know what to expect if'n he reaches Nogales.'

'What we gonna do, Jack?' asked the kid. 'Leave here now and that's the last we'll see of that dough.'

Vandyke was ready with the solution to their problem. 'The four of us could set up an ambush at a place I know if'n we leave right away. Get rid of him then you can give me my share of the dough and we can call it quits.'

'Seems a mighty large share for just one extra gun hand,' Greylag prevaricated.

'Without my help, you guys won't know which way he's coming. A guy like that can spot trouble in his sleep.' He leaned back, lighting up a cheroot. 'If'n you're figuring that three guns are enough to handle Iron Matt Devlin, think again. You've heard about his reputation, Jack. Tell this turkey.'

'He's right there, boys. Devlin is reckoned to be the tops in that game.' Vandyke suppressed a snort of anger. 'But what you ain't cottoned to, fella, is the fact that Henry Douglas, that teamster, is toting the haul from the Willcox job in his wagon.'

'So you ain't got it stashed away around here then?' Vandyke spluttered, unable to conceal the shock such an earth-shattering announcement had caused.

'That's what I said, ain't it?' Patch leaned close in to the Dutchman, a malevolent warning patently evident in his next remark. 'So if'n you were hoping to grab the dough for yourself . . .'

Vandyke sat back, raising his arms. 'The thought never crossed my mind. All I want is to help you fellas get rid of Devlin — for a small consideration, of course.'

'Just so's you got the message,' added Klute, flexing his narrow shoulders, 'we don't help charity cases. If'n you come in with us, it better be worth the payout.'

Patch nodded in accord. Having made his point, he continued. 'Nobody would ever suspect a milksop like Douglas of carrying all that dough. Good thinking, eh?' He smiled at his own shrewdness, even though it had been Jim Smollett's idea. 'But we have to wait around here until he arrives.'

Vandyke's irate look went unheeded

as the outlaws considered their predicament. It was true what Patch had asserted. All that time he was with the wagon, and never once had he ever suspected that the strong box was within easy reach. He tipped a hefty belt of tequila down his throat to dull the pain of hindsight. At that moment, Dutch Geery Vandyke was not a happy man.

Yet he could still come out of this with a smile on his kisser. 'How about if'n me and these guys head out to waylay Devlin while you stay here and wait for Douglas to arrive? Reckon I know just the place to set up an ambush.'

11

Ambush

Patch had taken some convincing that the new guy's plan was the best way forward. He trusted the Dutchman like he would a rabid dog. But with the resurrection man riding alongside the wagon containing their loot, that spelled double trouble. And Vandyke was slick when it came to arguing the toss.

'Believe me, Jack,' he insisted, 'this is the only way to get the guy off'n our backs.'

It appeared that he was right. Patch could see no other way forward.

The two robbers in company with Geery Vandyke left Nogales soon after.

Around noon of the following day, they were waiting in the rocks overlooking an open sward of sand. The only cover out there was a small clump of jumping cane and some creosote bushes. This was the spot the Dutchman had judged to be the perfect place for an ambush. Plenty of rocky cover to conceal the bushwhackers when their quarry emerged from the confines of the narrow canyon down which he would surely have to come.

'How long do we have to wait?' asked the sceptical Klute. 'The guy could have taken a different route. We could be pissing into wind just sitting around here.'

They had only been there for a half hour and already the kid was bleating.

'Trust me,' Vandyke muttered in a deliberately puerile voice as if he were berating a slow child. 'I know this guy, how he thinks. This is the route he'll take. His whole being is eaten up with getting even with the critters that raped and murdered his wife. Remember? So he won't want to waste any time getting his revenge. He knows you're all meeting up in Nogales. And this is the quickest route for a horse and rider.' Vandyke was deliberately rubbing Klute's nose in his own mess. It was because of him the ex-bounty hunter was on their case.

'He could be hours yet. That is if'n he comes at all. I'm having a smoke.'

'No, you ain't,' Vandyke ordered. 'You want to reveal our presence here? Have a bit of sense and put the makings away. And act your age for once.'

'Don't you damned well order me around, mister,' Klute retorted angrily. 'You're the new boy in this outfit so quit pushing your luck.'

'Button your lip, kid, before I put you over my knee.'

The Dutchman's acidic reply was taken up by Greylag who was no less derisive of his associate. 'Do as he damned well says, Klute, and shut the heck up else I'll bury you myself. What the boss was thinking when he took on a snivelling brat like you, I don't know. We come out of this unscathed, I'm cutting loose. Working with snotty kids is for teachers.' The older guy was becoming well and truly worked up. His face had turned purple. The mood of bitter resentment had clearly been festering for some time past. 'Jack should have dumped you long ago. You're nothing but a lame duck.'

The virulent tirade was too much for Klute. A snarl of hate bellied up from deep within his scrawny frame. The Winchester carbine swung towards the source of the cutting invective. Age had slowed Greylag down. He stood no chance against a young gunny like Klute.

Before Vandyke could make a move to stymie the rash deed, two slugs had punched the old guy back. His own shooter had barely cleared leather. The punctured torso slid down the rock wall where he'd been standing, leaving a streak of red in its wake.

'You durned fool,' railed Vandyke impotently. 'Why couldn't you kill the old turnip after we've done what we came for? That's another man less for

Devlin to deal with. And if'n smoking didn't do it, like as not those shots will have given him warning of our position.'

'Nobody speaks to me like that and lives,' the kid growled back, his gun swinging to cover the Dutchman. 'You'd do well to remember that as well, mister. Anyway, that old soak weren't no loss. A grizzled has-been. And with him out the way, there's more dough for the rest of us.' The ugly smirk was cold as the desert at night.

'You're a regular caring guy, ain't you, Klute?' The heavy dose of irony was completely lost on the kid. 'Always thinking of the other fella. It's real heart-warming to know you're on my side.'

Klute nodded, accepting the apparent climb down. 'Glad you feel that way, Geery. You're one smart dude. So let's forget about Greylag and concentrate on removing this God-watcher once and for all.'

The Dutchman was temporarily

awestruck by this reckless braggart's effrontery. But it was only fleeting. There was work to be done. And a fresh plan of action needed to be rehashed straight away.

'We'll need to split up.' Vandyke now took charge of the new logistics of the ambush. 'My guess is that Devlin is bound to have heard those shots. So we'll use Greylag as bait to lure him into the open.'

He then went on to explain what he had in mind.

Klute was decidedly nervous when his part in the subterfuge was outlined. 'I ain't too sure about acting as decoy. That guy could just haul off when he sees me standing over the body.'

Vandyke shook his head. He was adamant that no such thing would happen. 'Matt ain't that kind of guy. Especially since he took to preaching. He'll give you a fair shake, the chance to surrender. And that's when I take him down.'

'How long do you figure it'll be afore

he turns up?' Klute had become much more diffident since his shooting of Greylag, He had simmered down, comprehending the seriousness of their situation.

'My guess is anytime soon,' the Dutchman asserted, keeping a wary eye on the exit from the canyon on the far side of the clearing. 'So we need to set things up, pronto.'

A jack rabbit scampered across the open sward, disappearing into a hole. Nothing else moved. The sun beat down relentlessly. Its heat was intense within the confines of the rocky enclave. Vandyke unscrewed the lid of his water bottle and took a long swig. He wiped the sweat from his brow. The kid didn't seem to feel the heat.

Well, that was about to change big time.

Once they had carried the dead body out into the open, Klute was becoming decidedly edgy about his role in the forthcoming piece of deception.

'Why can't we just leave Greylag out

in the open?' he posited, being less than eager to expose himself to the wrath of this avenging angel.

But Vandyke was ready with an answer. 'He sees a body lying there alone, it'll make him suspicious, hold him back from putting himself in the firing line. But with you out there, he'll reckon to have caught the culprit red-handed. And with his attention fully focused on you, I'll be able to chop him down from up here.'

There didn't appear to be any further argument available to the anxious gunslick. 'Just make sure that your aim is perfect,' Klute nervously implored his associate.

'Easy as shooting tin cans off a fence,' the grinning Dutchman assured him. 'Now you get down there. And make it look good.'

Vandyke had been right when he said that his nemesis would have heard the gunfire. Matt had only left the Douglas wagon a half hour before he drew his horse in and listened. There were no further shots, just the two. Could Shonto still be lurking in the area on the hunt for fresh scalps? The shots had come from up ahead. Some other poor traveller might be in trouble. There was only one way to find out. He spurred off, galloping between the clutching ranks of broken rock. Within fifteen minutes, he emerged from the canyon to see a gunman bending over a body lying on the ground.

Gun in hand, Matt immediately recognized the boyish features of the outlaw known as Klute.

'Don't make no sudden moves, kid,' he snapped, sliding effortlessly out of the saddle. Gun hand steady as a rock, he approached the jittery desperado. 'Looks like it's four down with two to go seeing as how you've removed this old coot from the picture for me.'

'Don't shoot, mister. We had an argument and he tried to gun me down. I was only protecting myself,' Klute blustered. The sweat now coating his brow was from real fear. His eye strayed towards the rocks on the far side of the clearing where his sidekick was hiding.

The hesitant move was immediately spotted by the avenger. His brain clicked into place. Instantly he knew it was a set-up with him as the easy target. He moved to one side just as Vandyke pulled the trigger of his Winchester. But the move to save himself came too late. Arms were flung wide. Nerveless fingers clutched air before he tumbled to the ground.

Klute stood there transfixed, his whole body trembling. 'Boy, that was close, too darned close,' he muttered under his breath. His chest heaved. All he could do for the moment was stare at the fallen body. Was it really all over? Could he breathe again?

'You done well, boy,' a deadpan voice behind drawled out. 'Give yourself a pat on the back. Pity it'll be the last thing you do.' A macabre guffaw followed. 'Apart that is, from shaking hands with the Scythe Man.' The blood drained from Klute's face as he spun on his heel. Facing him was the ugly grimace of Death. Once again the Winchester spat lead. And another gunslinger bit the dust.

This was turning out much better than Dutch Vandyke could ever have wished for. His old foe removed at a stroke along with two of the robbers. All in a single action. And carried through slick as you please. Now all he had to do was head back to Nogales and await the coming of the Douglas wagon. The only thing then standing in his way and the $30,000 would be Jack Patch.

Self-assurance oozed from every orifice of the sly gun-toter. He was sure that somewhere along the trail he could remove that final obstacle to a life of luxury. And so with a gleam in his eye and skip in his step, Geery Vandyke returned to his horse. The future was looking decidedly rosy.

Matt Devlin had not been the only one to hear the gun shots. The wind was blowing in the right direction. Sharp reports could much more easily be picked up by acute ears.

'Hear that, Henry?' Laura Douglas gripped her husband's arm.

Instinctively she sensed that the paladin so recently escorting them was the object of the violence. 'It's Mr Devlin. He's in trouble.'

'You don't know that, woman. And anyway, what can we do about it?' Henry asked with too casual a shrug. 'This wagon can't take the trail he took.'

But Laura was adamant. 'It's him. I know it is. That gunslinger Vandyke must have been lying in wait for him. He could be bleeding to death out there. We have to do something. He was good to us. Helped us out when we needed it most. Least we can do is repay his consideration.'

Douglas was becoming exasperated. 'We can't do nothing, Laura. Guys that live by the gun, die by it.'

'How can you be so callous about a man who gave all that up?' the woman rebuked her man scornfully. 'His wife

185

was killed by a gang of heartless brutes.' Her back stiffened as she drew away. 'I'm taking the spare horse to go find him. You stay here and make an early camp.'

Douglas was about to remonstrate. But the frosty look in his wife's eyes stayed the intended dissension. When Laura was in this stubborn frame of mind, nothing would sway her. Another shrug. 'Have it your own way,' he muttered. 'I just hope you don't land yourself in hot water cos I won't be able to help if'n you do.'

Laura was not listening. Already, she had jumped off the wagon and was saddling up the horse. Seeing his wife about to ride off into the unknown made Henry Douglas realize how much he loved her. 'Take this gun,' he said, offering her a small Marston threeshot pocket pistol. 'It ain't much. But you need something more than plain sassiness going out there alone.'

Her manner softened. The smile that lit up her face warmed his heart. 'It's the right thing to do, Henry.'

He nodded. 'Just make sure you come back.'

Then she was gone, disappearing behind a stand of cottonwoods.

12

Confession

Heading in the general direction from which the shots had originated, Laura prayed hard that she would not lose herself amidst the wild terrain. But mostly that she would be in time to help the gun-fighting preacher who had so upset her ordered life. There could be no denying now that she felt something more than mere concern for the man's welfare.

Even for a town bred woman like Laura, following the trail of hoof prints through the meandering wilderness was straightforward. Only one set had passed this way, and recently, judging by their clear-cut impression in the sand. On and on she rode, impatient to discover the grim reality of the gun shots. Orange blocks of rock hemmed her in on all sides, their remarkable shapes the result of scouring by wind-blown sand. The experience could have been daunting for any ordinary female. But Laura Douglas had a fixed purpose from which there could be no deviation.

Circumvention of a lofty promontory while exiting the strict confines of the narrow canyon brought her face to face with death in all its brutal finality. A cry of anguish issued from her ashen face. The sudden revelation brought on by the awful sight almost made her faint. Somehow she managed to swallow down the nausea welling up in her throat.

Ignoring the two other bodies, she had eyes only for the one man she recognized. A buzzard was perched on the still form. The curved beak of the predator was ready to tear and rip the tasty flesh from the bone. Laura jumped off her horse, arms flapping like a demented rooster.

Desperation lent added vigour to the

ungainly ploy as she drove the creature away before it could inflict any damage. An angry cawing was her reward as the buzzard lifted skywards.

She hurried across. Fear displayed in her watery gaze became all the more terror-stricken on seeing the dried blood caking his head.

'Please, please,' she shouted aloud to the God she had ignored for too long. 'Let him be alive.'

Dropping to her knees, she gently cradled the still body in her arms. Time stood still as she rocked back and forth. Then a miracle happened. A groan issued from between cracked lips before he lapsed once again into unconsciousness.

But it was enough. Laura's eyes lifted to the Heavens. 'Thank you, thank you,' she croaked. But there was no time to lose. He was clearly at death's door. God helps those who help themselves was what her mother had always professed. She carefully laid him down and rushed back to her horse, breathing a sigh of relief at her foresight in collecting the canteen and medical box before leaving the wagon.

Ten minutes later, the wound had been cleaned and disinfected. A bullet had scored a furrow along the left side of Matt's head, which was now swathed in a bandage. Another half inch and his brains would have been splattered across the sandy wasteland. Laura didn't think about that. He was alive, that was the main thing. She dribbled water between the parched lips.

A further ten minutes passed before Matt regained consciousness. His eyes flickered open to reveal a smiling angel peering down at him. 'Am I in Heaven?' he groaned, attempting a smile that resulted in a pained grimace.

'Another couple of minutes and you would have been,' Laura replied, pointing to the repulsed scavenger watching from a safe distance. 'You need to rest up now.'

The patient was not about to argue with such a comely nurse. Once again his eyes closed. Laura removed her coat and laid it across him for protection against the sun's relentless heat. More time elapsed before she would allow him to stand up. Leaning on her shoulder, he was able to stagger across to rest in the shade of a rocky overhang. And there he lay, slowly replaying the events that had led to the ambush.

'Those two critters over yonder were with Jack Patch. So whoever gunned me down must have done for them as well.' His rheumy eyes misted over. 'And I have a good idea who that was.' Laura stroked his head, waiting. 'Has to be Geery Vandyke. The rat must have teamed up with Patch. He wants that strong box and has no intention of sharing the proceeds with anyone else. Jack Patch is in for one helluva surprise.' A mirthless smile flickered across the ashen features. 'Both those critters will be under the mistaken assumption I've been removed from the picture. Big mistake on their part. And one that gives me a distinct edge.'

When he felt strong enough, Laura helped Matt clamber up on to his horse. Together they slowly retraced their steps back to the camp where Henry Douglas was waiting on tenterhooks. It was with mixed feelings that he greeted the arrival of the wounded man.

A cup of hot coffee laced with whiskey was pushed into Matt's hand. He drank it down gratefully.

'Boy, that tastes like the nectar of the Gods. The Big Guy sure has been smiling down on me today. And he sent one of his angels to watch over me.' This latter remark was uttered in a hushed whisper so that Douglas could not hear. Laura smiled. But her concerned regard was for a recuperating patient.

Over supper, Matt was becoming increasingly aware that Henry Douglas was concealing something. The guy was continuing to act in a shifty manner that had nothing to do with any danger from the Apaches. He had spoken barely a word since his return. A few general enquiries, inane trivia, but barely a mention of the ambush.

Matt studied him closely across the dancing embers of the fire. Dodgy looks were cast his way as the guy puffed hard on his cheroot. His nervousness was even more pronounced now than when he had decided to leave them and head direct for Nogales. There was some issue bugging Douglas and it needed bringing out into the open.

Laura had also noticed her husband's detached manner. She put it down to her husband being jealous of this handsome stranger coming into their lives. Trying to ignore a sense of unease, she fussed about tidying the dishes away. Matt continued arrowing a caustic frown at her husband. A tension you could cut with a knife was surely building to an ugly confrontation.

Matt tossed the dregs of his cup into the fire and lurched to his feet. He stood menacingly over the cringing teamster.

'If'n you have something on your mind, Henry, I want to know.' Douglas prevaricated fruitlessly, trying to dismiss the accusation. But Matt was having none of it. 'There's more to it than Indians and Vandyke so don't deny it. You have some beef with me, then let's hear what it is.'

Douglas lowered his head. He sucked in a deep breath. The moment for divulgence of his subterfuge had arrived. 'You're right,' he murmured softly. 'There is something I need to get out into the open. And it ain't good news.'

Matt stiffened. A quick glance was exchanged between himself and the woman. Was he about to voice his accusation regarding Matt's innermost turmoil? They both waited uneasily. What emerged was a confession that neither of them could ever have foreseen in a million years. Mind blowing to say the least.

The man swallowed, shifting about uneasily. His next words were directed towards his wife. 'I've been in cahoots with the Patch Gang since they robbed that Express Office in Willcox.' Laura's large eyes opened with surprise. 'Not only that, we're carrying the loot here in the wagon. The strong box is hidden under the seat. And inside is thirty grand in used bills.'

The admission was received in mesmerized silence. It was barely creditable to Matt that all this time he had been acting as guardian to the stolen plunder. He shook the notion from his head. Laura was equally stunned by the revelation. And it was genuine. Matt could see that the woman was not play-acting. She harboured not the faintest inkling that her husband had joined forced with a gang of owlhoots.

'I had no idea,' she blurted out. The denial was as much for their protector as her husband. 'What made you do such a thing? Henry Douglas, my husband, a common thief?' She turned away to hide her chagrin.

The guilty man now desperately tried to justify his actions. 'There was no way we could start up afresh in Nogales without a proper stake. When one of Patch's men offered me a thousand bucks to carry the dough for him, I jumped at the chance.' His hand reached out to the woman. But she cringed away from his touch. 'I know now that it was wrong. If'n I'd known at the start I was getting involved with a bunch of cold-hearted killers, don't you think I would have refused?'

Laura now deigned to address her man. The scornful look she gave him turned the poor man's face white. 'Would you, Henry, would you really? I don't know anymore. You're not the man I married, the man I fell in love with. The Henry Douglas I married had scruples, a sense of right and wrong. Where did that go?'

'I knew how you would react if'n I told you. And I was right. That was why I kept it from you.'

'Can you blame me for being angry?'

In truth, Laura was more upset about having been duped by the man she had trusted.

Once again, a conspicuous silence descended over the small group huddled around the campfire. It gave Matt time to consider a course of action to pursue. 'So what now, Douglas? You still hoping to complete your part of the deal?' Matt felt like he had just received the confession of a recalcitrant parishioner.

The acknowledged offender shook his head. 'It was weak-willed, I know, allowing myself to be hooked in by these crooks. The lure of easy money is a hard mistress to deny. But now that I've come clean, I feel like a great weight has been lifted from my shoulders.' He looked at his wife, silently begging her forgiveness. 'I hope you believe me, Laura, and that we can make a fresh start. That's why I've told you before it's too late.'

The woman did not respond. Instead, she swung on her heel and walked away, not bothering to hide the disdain that gripped her heart. She needed time to think, time to ponder on what had to be done. A low sigh from the desert wind rustled the leaves of the palo verde trees, as if in communion with her dilemma.

'It's been like a maggot eating away at my insides,' Douglas admitted to the stoic guardian while his pain-filled eyes followed his wife who continued walking up and down, trying to get her head round the unsettling admission.

When she finally returned to the wagon, Douglas once again tried to gain her understanding. But still Laura maintained an aloof coolness. She was not about to let him off the hook that easy. The distraught man just sat there, his shoulders slumped in shameful ambiguity.

Matt, however, knew exactly what had to be done. And he voiced his judgement in no uncertain terms.

'Patch is expecting you to arrive in Nogales in a couple of days to hand over the box. That right?' Douglas offered a gloomy nod of agreement. 'Well, I can't allow that to happen.' He fixed a determined look on the confessor. 'And I guess you've arrived at the same conclusion, seeing as how you've spilled the beans.'

'So what should I do?'

'Take your wife . . . ' Matt looked to the stiff form of Laura Douglas. ' . . . that is if'n she'll still support you.' He waited for the woman to respond. All he received was a lackadaisical shrug. At least it wasn't a downright refusal. Douglas perked up, sensing there was still hope for them. 'My advice is for you to make a fresh start someplace else. Far away from Nogales as possible. When Patch gets the message that you aren't going to turn up, he'll be hopping mad and come a-looking for you. But all he will find is me. And I ain't about to surrender this dough to anybody other than the authorities.'

The cold mask of determination on

Matt's face offered no alternative. This was how it was going to play out. Whatever the outcome. Jack Patch was the last of the six men who had defiled his wife and turned his own life on its head. It would be a showdown to the finish. Only one would walk away. As for Geery Vandyke — Matt touched the bandage swathing his head — he had thrown his lot in with the Devil and would pay the price for his folly.

13

The Mouse that Roared

Another couple of days passed before Matt felt well enough to make his stand against Patch and Vandyke. Laura was dubious. The drawn features, gaunt and blotchy, were proof that her concerns were valid. 'You are still far too weak to take on a couple of determined desperadoes and live to tell the tale.'

But he was adamant. Nothing was going to prevent him from finally coming face to face with the cause of all his anguish. He ignored her plea to exercise circumspection.

'Reckon it's about time you folks were leaving,' he declared flatly. 'Toss me down that strong box, Henry.'

Laura threw up her arms in frustration. 'Men,' she spat out scornfully.

202

'You're all so mule-headed. Always having to prove you have what it takes even if that means a bullet in the guts. I wash my hands of you.'

Nevertheless, Laura made sure to leave sufficient supplies to tide him over during the waiting period. The strong box was placed out in the open where it could not be missed while Matt moved his campsite into the cover of some rocks hidden away from view.

Douglas also voiced his wariness about leaving Matt alone, much to Laura's surprise. 'Me and Laura can both use rifles. Why don't we stay here and support you. One wounded man against two armed and determined villains hell bent on grabbing this dough are long odds.'

'I appreciate your concern for my welfare,' Matt replied with genuine accord, 'both of you. But this is my battle. And I don't want you folks getting in the way. No offence, Henry. But you ain't no gunslinger. And I don't want to be responsible for your safety. Best thing all round is for you to disappear.' An expressively affecting regard was reserved for Laura. She responded with an understanding smile. 'Forget you ever heard of me or Jack Patch. West of here you'll likely meet up with Lieutenant Thorough-good and his patrol. They can escort you back to Benson.'

Douglas did not argue. He was secretly relieved that his offer had been refused. But Laura knew that she could never forget this enigmatic stranger. Nor did she want to.

She gently took hold of his hand and squeezed it. 'I won't ever forget what you've done for us, Reverend Matt Devlin.' Then she climbed up on to the wagon next to her husband.

'All we can do now is wish you luck,' Douglas averred, unaware of the silent communication that had passed across the ether. 'It's due to you that I've seen the light. Perhaps there is a god up there looking out for us after all.'

Then he whipped up the team which

lurched into motion.

Only once did Laura turn around. Matt stood there in the clearing, a dark silhouette starkly etched against the bright orange rock, solid and unmoving. A man alone facing his destiny. Moments later, the steadfast figure disappeared from view. Had he truly gone from their lives forever?

★ ★ ★

The wagon reached the crossroads a couple of hours later. Faded signboards gave directions — north to Benson, south west to Nogales. Henry drew to a halt. For some moments, he stared hard at the lone tree and its indicators. His ribbed brow told of indecision clouding his mind.

'What's the matter, Henry?' his wife enquired, instantly picking up on the quandary. 'Why have we stopped?'

Henry didn't respond. Instead he swung the team towards the south west, and Nogales. Laura stiffened.

'What are you doing?' Panic registered in her trembling reaction. 'Benson lies in the opposite direction.'

'We're not going to Benson. I'm through with being faint-hearted.' His voice was firm and decisive, his shoulders set square and resolute. 'The old Henry Douglas has gone, buried back in that canyon. We're heading for Nogales where I intend giving myself up to the law. That guy back there deserves more than me just slinking away with my tail between my legs. This way I can at least prove there's still grit left in Henry Douglas's backbone and not water.'

Laura was momentarily stunned. But pride in her husband's unexpected transformation revealed itself when she leaned over and kissed him on the cheek.

'Then let's not waste any more time,' she concurred, snuggling close up and feeling the latent strength of purpose embracing them both. 'As I recall, we're both in this together.'

Henry slapped the reins and cracked the whip. He was feeling a new man. The trail to Nogales was direct and clear. Two days' ride to the south west.

'Let's both offer a prayer up that Shonto and his bunch have moved on,' he murmured, casting a bleak eye across the rolling arid terrain. 'Last thing I need now is a haircut.' He tried to make light of the gruesome possibility.

Laura laughed along with him. The new Henry was like a breath of fresh air. 'If'n they do try anything, husband,' she resolutely maintained, 'we'll give them a reception they won't forget in a hurry.' She gripped her rifle tighter.

★   ★   ★

At the end of the trail, Jack Patch was restively expectant as he awaited the return of his associates. He was seated in the Picador, the contents of a bottle of whiskey steadily disappearing down his throat.

'Where in tarnation are those critters?' he kept mumbling to himself. He had positioned himself with a good view along the main street where he could eyeball any newcomers entering the town from the north.

The grim expression, the disturbing mood emanating from the one-eyed brigand kept all the other customers well clear. His gang was being whittled down. And now he was dependent on a spineless wagon driver and a devious gunslinger to come out of this disaster with something to show for his angst. It was not a good position into which a guy wanted to find himself.

He cursed aloud, slamming the bottle down on the table top. 'Where in hell's name are you turkeys?' he railed, causing the encircling crowd to shrink further back. Then he saw him. Geery Vandyke riding down the street. But he was alone. Where in blue blazes were Greylag and Klute?

Jumping up, he dashed outside to confront the returning emissary. 'What the hell happened? Where are the other two?'

'Give me a drink first,' the lone rider shot back. 'Then I'll tell you.'

Struggling to maintain a cool head, Patch led the way back into the saloon and across to his table. Vandyke took a long slug then slumped into a chair. He was bushed. Yet not too tuckered out to make Jack Patch squirm with impatience. 'Which do you want first, the good news or the bad?'

Patch snarled. 'Don't play games with me, fella. Just spit it out.'

But the Dutchman was not to be hurried, nor intimidated. He had the whip hand and knew it. He lit up a cigar and took another slug of whiskey, leaving Patch fuming in impotent fury. But there was nothing he could do.

'The bad news is that Klute and Greylag won't be joining us.'

The blood drained from Patch's face. His jaw dropped. 'You mean they're both . . . '

'That's exactly what I mean,' Vandyke

said. 'That preacher jumped us. Caught us out in the open. He sure is a crack shot. Took out Greylag and the kid with a single bullet for each of them. I was lucky being at the back of the queue and managed to dive behind a handy boulder.'

'So what's the good news?' A morose regard did not anticipate a welcome deliverance. 'Apart from you coming out of the fracas untouched. If'n that can be regarded as good.'

Vandyke ignored the caustic retort. He paused and drew on a cigar, leaving Patch disgruntled and still floundering like a landed fish. 'The critter didn't have it all his own way. I left him there for the buzzards to chew on. He won't be bothering us no more.'

Then he sat back, allowing Patch to absorb the import of his revelations. It was Jack who needed another drink now. But the bottle was empty. He signalled across to the barman for another.

'Devlin is strumming with the angels?'

he pressed. 'You certain about that?'

'Got him in the head. He's a goner all right.'

A fresh gleam of hope found Patch's gaunt features flushed with anticipation. 'So all we have to do is wait on the arrival of Douglas and the wagon carrying the dough.' A fist pounded the open palm of his hand. At last something good appeared to be emerging from this fiasco.

'My proposal is that we meet him along the trail,' Vandyke submitted. 'That way we don't have any varmints sticking their noses where they ain't welcome. I've seen too many guys hanging around this berg who would like nothing better than a free payout. We need some privacy when that strong box is offloaded.'

Patch was all for that. 'Good thinking, Dutch. I reckon in that case we ought to hit the trail purty soon.'

Vandyke had not been shamming when he claimed to be tired. He was no spring chicken and the high jinks of the last week or so had left him jaded. 'I need some sleep,' he slurred, yawning and stretching his arms. Patch tried protesting, but the Dutchman would not be swayed.

'That wagon won't be here for another two days. Plenty of time to waylay it on the trail.' And with that he stood up. 'I'll bunk down in your room.' He held a hand out for the key.

Patch reluctantly complied. 'I'll wake you at first light. Be ready to ride.'

Early next morning, the two brigands were riding out of Nogales just as the sun was climbing above the prominent cone of Miller Peak on the eastern horizon. Geery Vandyke was well rested and raring to put some distance behind him. They kept up a steady canter all morning, only stopping for brief intervals once every hour. Accordingly it was around noon when they reached the approximate halfway point between Nogales and the crossroads.

And that was when they came across the lone wagon. The two brigands pulled off the trail behind a couple of towering saguaro cacti and waited for the wagon to arrive. As it drew near, they emerged from cover, much to the surprise of the occupants.

'Glad to see you made it, Douglas,' Patch greeted their arrival with enthusiasm. 'Just toss the box down so I can check that all the dough is there. Then I can pay you off and we'll split the breeze. A job well done.'

Vandyke pulled back. The hard beetling look on his face did not auger well for such a share out. His hand slid towards the gun on his hip. Then he received a shock that no amount of planning could have predicted.

'I don't have it.' The blunt denial from Henry Douglas saw both men visibly stiffening. The animated grin cloaking Patch's warped face slipped as the driver explained his predicament. 'It's back yonder with the Reverend Devlin. And he's waiting on you guys to try and take it from him.'

Vandyke was the one most stunned

by this shock announcement. 'But I left him for dead,' he spluttered, unable to comprehend the guy's claim. 'You're lying.'

'No, he ain't!' Laura butted in. 'You gunned him down all right. But I heard the shots and managed to save his life.' A manic laugh bubbled over as the woman warmed to her eye-opening disclosure. 'That's sure gotten you in a stew, ain't it? Turned the tables on your odious scheme good and proper.'

'We're heading for Nogales to report the whole matter to the sheriff,' Douglas declared with a firm positive assurance. 'I might spend time in Yuma. But it'll be worth it to regain some self-respect.' He raised the whip in readiness to urge the team back on to the move.

Patch now found his voice. And he was hopping mad. His face mushroomed in a dark cast that did not bode well for the driver's health. 'Why, you double-crossing skunk.' His gun was palmed in the blink of an eye. Orange flame and smoke belched forth as three bullets, one after the other, drilled the teamster dead centre. It was a sudden and brutal termination of his new found tenacity. There would be no further salving of Henry Douglas's conscience this day or any other.

Laura screamed. She raised her own rifle to avenge her brave husband's death. But Vandyke grabbed hold of her around the waist, dragging her to the ground.

'I have some other plans for you, Mrs Douglas. You're gonna be my ticket to the good life. I saw the way that God-blasted preacher looked at you. Ain't no doubt in my mind that he'll surrender that dough knowing what a refusal would mean.' He grabbed her hair, yanking her head back. A frenzied leer found the terrified woman cringing away. But she was held in an iron grip. 'Now get back up there and turn this heap around,' he snapped, pushing her roughly towards the wagon.

The two desperadoes climbed into

the bed of the wagon hidden from view. Patch had quickly cottoned on to his associate's plan. 'A wrong move, missy, and you'll be joining that damned turncoat,' he snarled. 'Now get this team moving. Enough time's been wasted. And I want that dough in my saddle-bags before sundown.'

The menacing curl of Vandyke's lip told of a very different outcome. One that did not include Patch. But he would keep that piece of wisdom to himself until a suitable opportunity arose to dispose of his alleged partner.

Laura was shaking like a leaf. Even though a fierce sun was beating down, her whole body felt chilled to the bone. One minute she and Henry were heading for a new beginning, the next he was gone and she was in her own version of Hell. And there was nothing she could do to help the one man who might have offered some form of justice to this dire situation.

'How much further?' Vandyke hissed after the wagon had been trundling along for a spell. Impatience showed itself in the acid rasp of his demand.

'Another couple of hours,' came back the tired response. 'It's on the far side of that hill.' The time had given her a chance to think, an opportunity to redeem some measure of defiance. 'He knows you're coming. Ain't no way Matt will let either of you critters off the hook.'

'Cut out the cackling, lady,' Patch growled. 'Your job is to drive the wagon. Ours is to get the dough.'

'And don't forget who's gonna be our secret weapon to the good life,' added the smirking Dutchman. 'Now quit mouthing off and get these nags on the move.'

14

And Then There Were . . .

Patch called a halt after an hour, ostensibly to relieve himself. 'Might as well brew up some coffee. There's no hurry. That varmint ain't going no place.' But his mind was on far more earthy needs. Vandyke had noticed how he kept ogling the woman. Licking his lips like a dog on heat. That knowledge gave him an idea.

'Mighty handsome woman, don't you reckon, Jack?' The whispered aside was for Patch's ears only. Those drooling eyes were all the answer he needed. 'Makes a fella go all kinda wobbly inside. Old Klute had the right idea when he took the preacher's wife. But all he got was a heap of trouble. Ain't nobody around here to object if some guy chose to exercise his passion.' He

218

stood up and sauntered away. 'I'll just take a walk and stretch my legs. Be gone about ten minutes. Time enough for you to keep Mrs Douglas company.'

'Yeah. You're right,' slavered the panting beast. 'See ya, buddy. No need to hurry back.' The wink was all Vandyke needed to know that his plan had well and truly taken root. From behind a nearby rock, he watched as the licentious Patch stumbled to his feet and moved up behind the unsuspecting female who was busy setting the coffee pot to boil. He unbuckled his gun belt and grabbed her around the waist, hauling her away from the fire.

'You and me's gonna have some fun, gal.'

Laura yelled out, struggling to extricate herself from the braggart's odious grip. But he was too strong. A back-hander across the face sent her tumbling to the ground. And there she lay, stupefied, barely able to comprehend what was about to happen.

'You'd do well not to fight me,' Patch

rasped, breathing heavily as the lust took a hold. 'Or it'll be you that gets hurt.' His hand rose to deliver another stunning blow.

That was when Vandyke made his presence felt. 'Now that ain't very gracious of you, Jack. Forcing yourself on a woman of such refinement. Guess you need a lesson in manners.'

Patch swung around, shock written across his ugly face. 'Keep outta this, Geery.'

The other man shook his head. 'Can't do that, Jack.'

Patch snarled a garbled curse then dived for his gun. But he stood no chance. Vandyke had him cold, literally with his pants down. His own shooter blasted. The poor man didn't stand a chance, spinning round like a child's top as another bullet ripped into the exposed torso.

The killer strolled across, blowing on the barrel of his revolver. 'And then there were none.' A mirthless grin broke across the twisted maw. 'Looks like it's only you and me left to face good old Iron Matt.'

The terrified woman cowered away, fearing this was yet another loathsome creature wanting to have his way with her. Vandyke raised his hands to show he wasn't about to repeat Patch's behaviour.

'You get to making that coffee, ma'am,' he assured her. 'That's all I'm wanting after all this excitement. With a snort of whiskey added to cool my nerves. Killing a man always leaves a fella kinda breathless for a spell.'

Sometime later, the wagon was back on the trail. Vandyke sat up front, keeping a sharp look out for anything suspicious. When he judged they were getting close to the scene of conflict, he concealed himself in the bed of the wagon.

'How far now?' he called, the tension evident in his clipped demand.

'Over that next rise,' came the subdued reply.

'You just keep going. And remember,

any funny business and this rifle is pointing straight at your back. We wouldn't want it to go off by accident now, would we?'

Looking over the woman's shoulder, the first thing he spotted once they had crested the hillock was the strong box lying in the sand, isolated and alone. The clearing was circular and surrounded by a low wall of rocks giving the impression of a gladiatorial arena of combat. And that was exactly what it would be, but with only one warrior lifting the trophy, in this case thirty grand, plus the woman.

Geery Vandyke had every intention that he would be that surviving combatant. There was no sign of Devlin which was only to be expected. He must have seen the wagon with the woman driving on her own and realized what had happened.

'Haul up, ma'am. And let me do all the talking.'

Ten minutes passed with no movement from either side. The breeze had dropped to a low murmur.

Not a single bird chirped or cavorted. No desert rats, not even a lizard deigned to make an appearance. Nothing invaded the field of conflict. It was as if all life forces that clung tenaciously to this forbidding land could sense the imminent confrontation and were holding their collective breath.

The Dutchman was the first to exhibit signs of frustration. 'Come on out, you goddamned Bible pusher,' he muttered to nobody in particular. 'Let's get this over with.'

Laura Douglas discerned the unease, the nervous trepidation now assailing her captor's entrails. And she intended milking it to the limit.

'You don't seem so eager to take on a real man face to face when the chips are down, Mr Vandyke,' she tossed back over her shoulder with a mocking snigger. 'Henry was more of a man than you'll ever be. And he proved it, right to the end.'

The scheming bounty hunter now

showed his true colours. The rifle jabbed viciously into her back. All his cool bravado evaporated like a splash of water in the desert. 'Best keep your purty mouth shut tight, gal, else I'll complete what that stupid Patch had in mind. Then I'll finish the job like what Klute did.'

Any further threats were cut short by a portentous voice that rang out from somewhere in the rocks on the far side of the amphitheatre. 'Guess I had you all wrong, Geery.' The declaration was flat, cold, devoid of emotion. 'Hiding behind a woman's skirts kinda suits your way of doing things.'

A macabre laugh floated back in response. The Dutchman was not to be goaded that easily. 'Why make things hard for myself, Devlin. I have the whip hand here and you know it. A simple trade off, that's all I want. The money for the woman. Easy as that. You think on it, Iron butt. But don't take too long. Mrs Douglas here is mighty fetching. I might decide to have some fun while I'm waiting on your call.'

Vandyke certainly knew how to dig the knife in deep. He had struck gold with that salacious remark.

'Harm one hair of her head and I'll hunt you down and string you up by the — '

'Better you didn't complete that toothless piece of claptrap,' Vandyke cut him off. 'Mrs Douglas would be exceedingly disappointed in her handsome paramour. Now I'm gonna walk over there slow and easy with this lady in front should you try anything foolish. I'll take the box and you can have the woman, and the wagon as a bonus seeing as how poor old Henry won't be tagging along. The clown unwisely figured he could report the theft to the sheriff in Nogales. We put an end to that nonsense. And then I did the same for Jack's ambitions. It's just you and me now, old sport.'

Matt was dumbfounded. So Douglas had refused to heed his advice and paid the ultimate penalty for his folly. An exceedingly rash decision, or one that proved he was far more plucky than previously assumed. It had gone against all sound common sense, although Matt couldn't deny the man had guts. In the final analysis, however, it had done him no favours. His main concern now was for the safety of Laura Douglas. So he made his anxiety abundantly clear. 'You all right, ma'am? This skunk ain't done you no harm, has he?'

'As fine as is possible under the circumstances,' she called back, even though it was clear from the trembling reply that the death of her husband had shaken her to the core. And who could blame her for that? It still left Matt with a dilemma.

Thankfully, he still had an ace up his sleeve.

A menacing guffaw greeted Vandyke's ears. 'You sure have been busy, punk. But you must think I'm wet behind the ears. Take a look and you'll find that strong box is empty. It was only put there to draw you in. I have the money right here in my saddle-bags.' He held off to let the other man assimilate the ramifications of his assertion. 'Now I suggest you leave right now while there's still breath left in that mangy frame. And alone. As a man of God I promise not to come after you. With Patch and his gang all pushing up the daisies, my job down here is finished. Don't make me add you to the list. My Boss might not be so forgiving.'

'No deal, preacher boy. I can't do that.' Vandyke's irate growl sounded like that from an angry bear. 'Too much water has passed under the bridge to stop now. All I want is that dough. Then I'll disappear. Now you toss your guns out into the open then follow them with those bags. We'll make the exchange in the middle of the clearing. Choose the wrong move and Mrs Douglas here joins her loving husband. Now you wouldn't want that, I'm sure, knowing how you feel towards her.'

Matt was seething. The truth always

hurt. But Vandyke's response came as no surprise. It was what he had expected all along. And it left him in a decidedly tricky position. 'What's to stop you gunning me down once you have the money?' he called back. 'That's what you've always wanted, isn't it, following that misunderstanding with Reb Dillard?'

'Misunderstanding! Who you trying to kid, buster? That was theft, pure and simple,' Vandyke barked on recalling the embarrassing incident. 'You're right, though. I should gun you down. But there's been enough killing already. So I'm prepared to trust you as a man of the cloth to keep your word and leave me alone when I ride out of here. Seems to me you ain't got no choice.'

'Don't listen to him, Matt,' Laura desperately pleaded. 'You can't put your trust in a rat like him. He won't shoot me. Guys like him ain't got the guts to shoot a woman.'

The brigand gripped her hair, a rasping threat hissing in her ear. 'Cut the griping, gal. I'm calling the shots here. And for your information, I'll do anything to get my hands on that thirty grand.' His next icy retort was for the hidden adversary. 'You hear that, Devlin? This ain't no game we're playing. The dame in exchange for the dough. You decide.'

Matt closed his eyes. With hands gripped tightly together, he prayed hard for guidance to do the right thing. For the courage needed to place his own life on the line to save that of another. The Lord had done the same thing at Calvary. Matt's face creased in shame. How could a simple pastor have the gall to compare his miserable situation to that ultimate sacrifice?

Moments later, a flash of forked lightning lit up the sky over the distant Dragoons. The startling portent was followed by a rumble of thunder. Now he had his answer.

Vandyke's threat was rewarded by seeing a Colt revolver and Winchester rifle being tossed out from behind a boulder. They were followed by the stoical figure of Iron Matt Devlin. In his right hand Matt held the heavy saddle-bags. Slowly, he made his way across the open sward. At the same time, Vandyke matched him step for step, pushing the female in front of him.

The killer scowled at his nemesis. The guy had a sickly grin pasted on his mouth. Devlin must have lost his marbles. It made his task all the easier.

'That's far enough,' the Dutchman ordered, pushing the woman roughly to the ground. 'Now drop the bags and step away.' Matt could only do as bidden. Satisfied that his stipulations had been adhered to, an ugly sneer now etched a path across the brigand's face. The hammer of his own revolver snapped back.

Matt stiffened. But he was impotent to do anything. Laura cried out, 'You promised to let him go free. All he ever wanted was to avenge the killing of his wife.'

'It was me that done most of that, lady. I never had any intention of letting him walk away. Guess he's known that all along. But good old Matt was always the chivalrous type. He just can't resist a lady in distress.' The sniggered remark was tainted with a heavy dose of sarcasm. 'And this is the final gesture.'

Laura sank to her knees, head in hands.

Vandyke responded with an uproarious cackle. 'So there we have it, lady. Your knight in shining armour is just that — all show and no teeth.' Another bellow of cynical delight. 'You sure were right about one thing, pal. I can't leave you here. Iron Matt Devlin never gives up. That was always your claim, wasn't it?. And I've no reason to figure it to be any different now. Let you go and I'd be forever looking over my shoulder, expecting that pious kisser to be standing there, gun in hand. As things stand, I can have the money, be rid of you and have the dame as well. Suddenly the future's looking much brighter for Geery Vandyke.'

Matt's face lifted to the Heavens as the killer's finger tightened on the trigger. 'Goodbye, sucker. See you in Hell!'

Another flash of lightning crackled as the heavens vented their wrath.

15

Shonto's Revenge

The pistol rose to deliver its deadly charge. Instead, the Dutchman's spine suddenly arched as he was thrown forward. Two arrows were sticking out of his back. The victim fell to the ground. Surprise registered on the skeletal features. But he still had enough strength to struggle back on to his feet.

The shaking gun hand rose to finish what it had started. Then a third arrow effectively terminated that ambition. Vandyke slumped to the ground and lay still.

The two intended victims of his heinous scheme were momentarily stunned by the abrupt reversal in their fortunes. The macabre spell was broken by the appearance of six mounted

Indians on the skyline. There they stood, unmoving, statuesque effigies sculpted by some primordial hand. Matt quickly moved across to the trembling woman and they clung together as the reality of their near death experience took hold.

Another Indian now stepped out from behind some rocks on the opposite side of the arena. He slung the bow around his shoulders, signalling to his men who rode down to join him leading a spare horse. The harbinger of death adjusted his black hat before mounting up. Together the band of warriors walked their ponies across to face the two spellbound white eyes.

Matt could not help wondering if they had just stepped out of the frying pan into the fire. For there, sitting astride his piebald pony, was none other than Shonto. The chief's intentions were impassive, unreadable. His manic gaze was fixed on to the body of the man he had just killed. Contemptuously he spat on it. Then, without uttering a word, turned, signalling for his men to depart.

Such behaviour was inconsistent with the Apache chief's regular actions. Death and destruction of those he blamed for stealing their tribal lands was normally of paramount importance. Why was he allowing these two members of the hated race of invaders to go untouched?

Matt needed to know. 'Wait, oh great Chief of the Mescaleros,' he appealed, stepping forward. 'Why have you killed this man and left us alone? We are most grateful for Shonto's intervention. But I need to know what has prompted you to exercise such mercy.'

The noble chief paused. His craggy profile offered no answers. The eagle feathers fastened to his bow quivered in the breeze as the cold gaze once again strayed to the dead body. Then a warped expression of fulfilment creased the weathered skin, an accusatory finger pointing at the punctured corpse.

'This piece of dung laid his dirty hands on my youngest daughter. After defiling her body . . . ' Tears welled in the great warrior's eyes. But his face remained inscrutable. Crying was for women. ' . . . he tied her to a tree and . . . ' Again emotion forced him to draw breath before resuming the anguished dialogue. ' . . . killed her with a knife. Not once but many times.'

Matt's eyes lifted. Now he understood. So that squaw whom Vandyke had besmirched was the daughter of this Apache chief. 'I am indeed sorry for Shonto's loss,' Matt sympathized. 'I also have suffered at the hands of white men. But not all of our race are against the Apache.'

The words passed over Shonto's head. He was not listening. Anger tinged with elation now caused his black eyes to glow like the embers of a fire. 'Now I am avenged. Manitou has spoken. So today I call a truce. You were to be this dog's next victims. Go in peace. But let it be known that the

Apaches have not abandoned their unswerving search for justice. The fight goes on.'

And with that final menacing promise, he and his men departed. Silently, the two survivors watched until the small band disappeared.

'I am not a drinking woman,' Laura declared, her chest heaving as the tension slowly drained away, 'but there are times when a shot of whiskey is all that will calm the nerves.'

She turned around and headed back to the wagon. Matt joined her and together they imbibed the amber nectar, toasting their good fortune at having come through the dicey experience relatively unscathed.

Matt offered a silent prayer up to his Maker for delivering him from the yoke of bondage called Revenge. They left the body of Geery Vandyke for the circling predators to feast on. This was no place to make camp. Climbing on to the wagon, Laura swung it around. She needed to return the way they had come to pick up the body of her husband.

'He deserves a proper burial in Nogales where we had hoped to settle down,' she said.

Matt concurred. He also had one further task that needed his attention. It concerned a promise made to a dying missionary. When they arrived back at the place where Henry Douglas lay, Matt saw that Jack Patch's horse was still grazing contentedly by the side of the trail on a clump of gramma grass. And there, strung round the saddle horn, was a sack. Tentatively, Matt felt inside. A solid object touched his searching fingers. He withdrew the solid gold Cross of San Xavier. A gasp of awe found Laura hurrying to his side.

The priceless icon glinted in the sunlight. 'It's beautiful,' she whispered. 'How did you know it was there?'

'A long story told to me by a dying priest,' he replied, eyes glued to the fascinating relic. 'I promised to return it to his church if'n I ever caught up with the thief. Geery Vandyke clearly had no idea what Patch was concealing.'

Side by side, they sat on the wagon, each wrapped in their own thoughts. There was much to mull over. Eventually talk emerged as to what the future might hold.

Laura was clear about her own intentions. 'With my share of the reward money, I aim to continue with Henry's ambition to create a freight hauling business. What about you? Are you going back to Firewall?'

Matt thought for a moment. He had secretly aspired to asking this woman to join him there. Sarah was gone. But life continued. And Laura Douglas would make a fine preacher's wife. But it appeared as if her future lay in a different direction. Tentatively he made a suggestion. 'If'n you ever find that freighting is not the life for you, I'd be obliged to show you around my parish back in the Santa Rosa Valley. It's a beautiful place and the folks are welcoming.'

Now it was Laura's turn to pause and consider. 'I might take you up on that, Reverend Devlin.' Her eyes misted over. 'I might just do that.' Then she kissed him on the cheek and the moment passed. 'Let's wait and see how destiny pans out.'

That was answer enough. A silent prayer of thanks drifted towards the firmament.

We do hope that you have enjoyed reading this large print book.

Did you know that all of our titles are available for purchase?

We publish a wide range of high quality large print books including:
Romances, Mysteries, Classics
General Fiction
Non Fiction and Westerns

Special interest titles available in large print are:
The Little Oxford Dictionary
Music Book, Song Book
Hymn Book, Service Book

Also available from us courtesy of Oxford University Press:
Young Readers' Dictionary
(large print edition)
Young Readers' Thesaurus
(large print edition)

For further information or a free brochure, please contact us at:
Ulverscroft Large Print Books Ltd.,
The Green, Bradgate Road, Anstey,
Leicester, LE7 7FU, England.
Tel: (00 44) **0116 236 4325**
Fax: (00 44) **0116 234 0205**

MASSACRE AT RED ROCK

Jack Martin

Liberty Jones is tired of war. Now he just wants to be left in peace, but trouble has a way of finding him. Riding into the town of Red Rock to escape a marauding tribe of Indians, any hopes of safety he had are soon dispelled. The town is under military command, facing a gathering of tribes who are determined to drive people from the town and reclaim their land. Liberty and his band of townspeople must face impossible odds before blood runs deep in the streets of Red Rock . . .